THE

STAGGERFORD

FLOOD

OTHER WORKS BY JON HASSLER

FICTION
Staggerford
Simon's Night
The Love Hunter
A Green Journey
Grand Opening
North of Hope
Dear James
Rookery Blues
The Dean's List
Keepsakes and Other Stories
Rufus at the Door and Other Stories

FOR YOUNG ADULTS
Four Miles to Pinecone
Jemmy

NONFICTION
My Staggerford Journal
Good People . . . from an Author's Life

THE

STAGGERFORD

FLOOD

❖

JON HASSLER

❖

VIKING

VIKING

Published by the Penguin Group

Penguin Putnam Inc., 375 Hudson Street, New York, New York 10014, U.S.A.

Penguin Books Ltd, 80 Strand, London WC2R 0RL, England

Penguin Books Australia Ltd, 250 Camberwell Road, Camberwell,
Victoria 3124, Australia

Penguin Books Canada Ltd, 10 Alcorn Avenue, Toronto, Ontario, Canada M4V 3B2

Penguin Books India (P) Ltd, 11 Community Centre, Panchsheel Park,
New Delhi—110 017, India

Penguin Books (N.Z.) Ltd, Cnr Rosedale and Airborne Roads, Albany,
Auckland, New Zealand

Penguin Books (South Africa) (Pty) Ltd, 24 Sturdee Avenue, Rosebank,
Johannesburg 2196, South Africa

Penguin Books Ltd, Registered Offices: Harmondsworth, Middlesex, England

First published in 2002 by Viking Penguin, a member of Penguin Putnam Inc.

1   3   5   7   9   10   8   6   4   2

LIBRARY OF CONGRESS CATALOGING-IN-PUBLICATION DATA
Hassler, Jon.
The Staggerford flood/Jon Hassler.
p.   cm.
ISBN 0-670-03125-9
1. Staggerford (Minn.: Imaginary place)—Fiction. 2. City and town life—Fiction.
3. Aged women—Fiction. 4. Friendship—Fiction.
5. Minnesota—Fiction. 6. Floods—Fiction. I. Title.
PS3558 A726 S73 2002
813'.54—dc21   2001056808

This book is printed on acid-free paper. ∞

Printed in the United States of America
Set in Bembo
Designed by Nancy Resnick

For Catherine, Geoff and Anna,
For Betsy and Chris, Mitchell and Maeve.
And for Emil

THE

STAGGERFORD

FLOOD

THIS YEAR

Because Agatha McGee's penmanship had become shaky with age, she relied on her younger friend Janet Meers to do her handwriting for her.

"Janet, are you coming into town today?" she asked over the telephone. "I have some invitations I'd like you to copy out for me and address the envelopes."

"Sure, what time?"

"Before two. Lillian comes over at two."

"I can come at eleven or one; take your pick."

"Come at eleven; we'll have lunch."

"Good, I'll bring sandwiches and soup."

Agatha protested, but not enough, fortunately, to sway Janet.

"What kind of sandwich would you like?" asked Janet.

"Tuna fish. But not in a bagel. Bagels are so hard to chew."

"Tuna on rye and bean soup. How's that?"

"That will be fine."

"What are the invitations for? Are you throwing a party?"

"I am, as a matter of fact."

A squeal of delight—"Oh, good!" Then, "Are Randy and I invited?"

"Never mind. You'll see when you get here."

Janet drove in from her split-level house on a scenic, wooded bend of the Badbattle River east of town. It was a lovely spring day.

Birds were kicking up a racket in the lime-green woods, and the roadsides were purple with violets. She entered town on the high end and coasted downhill to the Badbattle, noticing how harshly the sun lay across the sidewalks and doorways now that the elms had mostly been taken down. Everything—the lawns, the houses, the people out walking—seemed overexposed to the sky. Here and there an elm remained standing, but dying, partly dismantled by wind and woodpeckers, a stark and ugly monument to the shaded and graceful past.

She parked in front of Agatha's large white house that sat on the highest lot on River Street. She was glad to see that Agatha's nephew, Frederick Lopat, had finally finished repairing the shoulder-high retaining wall that kept her front yard from spilling into the street. She was pleased, too, having climbed the steps to the yard, to see that he had raked the grass and readied the small flower beds for the annuals he'd plant in a few weeks after the threat of frost was past. This morning he was painting the wrought-iron railing leading up to the front porch.

"Hi, Fredriko."

He turned to her with his customary nod and crooked smile, a paint brush in one hand, a small can of black Rust-Oleum in the other. He was a tall, pale, stoop-shouldered man in his fifties. His "Hi, Janet" was barely audible.

"Not working today?" she asked.

"I got plenty work around here."

"I mean in Willoughby."

"Nope, Saturday's my day off."

She held up the lunch bag she'd brought. "I've got your favorite here, ham and cheese."

"Good, thanks," he mumbled, and turned back to work.

She climbed to the wide front porch and pressed the doorbell.

"The bell's on the blink again," said Frederick. "Go ahead on in."

She did so, calling Agatha's name. There was no response. She called again, crossing the living room, and once again in the dining room. It occurred to her that Agatha may be dead. She glanced into the sunroom, then pushed open the swinging door into the kitchen with trepidation, half expecting to find Agatha, in her eightieth year, collapsed on the floor. She wasn't in the kitchen, but Janet shuddered anyhow, recalling the days before the flood when she had this expectation every time she approached this house. Before the flood Agatha didn't look well. She didn't act well. She spent whole days in her chair by the front window, brooding and watching the occasional car or pedestrian go by. The flood woke her up. The flood and her new pacemaker. The change was miraculous. She came out of the ordeal looking even smaller and more fretful than she had before, but a lot of her old energy came back, her erect posture, her strong voice, her fiery opinions.

Janet noticed the door to the enclosed back porch standing slightly ajar, and she found Agatha on the back stoop shaking out her dust mop. The woman seemed to have shrunk since she last saw her a month ago. Janet's daughter Sara, when she was in the fifth grade, was as tall as Agatha was now. She turned quickly to Janet, a sparkle of good humor in her small, lively eyes, because the sight of Janet always made her glad, and said, "Ah, there you are. Isn't it a perfect day? The sun actually is sending us down some warmth."

Bending to give the old woman a peck on the cheek, Janet agreed. "Spring is early this year. Most of our snow has already disappeared."

Agatha took her arm. "Yes, and the first thing I heard this morning was a pair of wrens. I came out here to verify it and saw one of them, so I've stopped worrying that winter might come back." She went on about birds while looking Janet over. She was pleased to see her hair cut short, no wrinkles yet except smile lines around her clear, steady eyes, and the frown mark in her forehead, the latter doubtless caused by worry concerning her husband, Randy, whom Agatha had never entirely approved of. "I thought they were orioles at first but orioles are cautious travelers, you know. They wait until it's completely safe before they come north and set up housekeeping."

With her eyes on the house across the alley, Janet said, "Lillian's place is still empty."

"It's not fit to live in. Because of the flood, you know."

"But that was almost a year ago. You mean it hasn't been repaired yet?"

"Nothing's been done. Empty ever since Imogene moved out. It's becoming an eyesore."

Lillian Kite's unmarried daughter, Imogene, as Janet knew, managed the local Carnegie Library. After the flood she had locked up the house and moved into a condo downtown. "Wouldn't you think they'd sell it?"

"It's not theirs to sell. It was usurped by the county commissioners months ago. *They* intended to sell it. To pay for Lillian's room at the Sunset Senior Home. But of course nobody wants damaged goods."

They stood there silent for a time, Janet's face raised to the warm sunshine, Agatha gazing at the house across the alley, recalling how, as a child, she used to watch for Lillian Kite out her kitchen window (this was before the back porch was added on). Lillian was Agatha's first and lifelong friend. Lillian's third birthday party was Agatha's first social occasion. She remembered how her anticipation turned to anxiety when she discovered Lillian's house full of three- and four-year-olds she'd never seen before. From the corners of rooms Agatha watched them screaming, wrestling, bursting balloons, and gorging themselves on popcorn and cake. Where did all these strangers come from and why was Lillian paying more attention to them than she was to Agatha? She cried. Mrs.

Kite sent word to Agatha's mother and she came and took her home.

But this party was not Agatha's earliest memory. Riding over the snow on a sled was the first event in her life she remembered. Her father had equipped the sled with a box to contain her and her blankets, and her mother was pulling her downtown through a gray afternoon to visit her father at his law office and to shop for groceries. They passed the houses of Mary Lou, Frankie, and Jenny Marie, children Agatha was not yet aware of and whose birthday parties she was destined, alas, to attend.

"Come, I'll show you the invitations before lunch," she said, rousing herself from her childhood reverie. "If we don't hurry I may change my mind. I've never been a party sort of person."

Sitting at Agatha's desk in the sunroom, Janet wrote half a dozen times,

Please grant me
the pleasure of your company
on April 14th
4 o'clock until 7 o'clock p.m.
in order that we may commemorate
our time together
during the Flood of the Century.
~Agatha

She then addressed the envelopes and joined Agatha and Frederick in the kitchen for lunch.

LAST YEAR

✦

THURSDAY

"I thought it was only Thursday," said Agatha. "I tell you, Lillian, I'm losing my grip."

"It *is* only Thursday."

"Well, see for yourself." Agatha pointed out her front window at the little red car at the curb, and at the man in a raincoat coming up the walk. "Saturday's his day."

"Oh, my," said Lillian, getting to her feet and tidying up the mess of cookie crumbs and dropped stitches on the lamp table beside her chair. Her needles and yarn she stashed into her JCPenney bag; the crumbs she brushed onto the carpet when Agatha wasn't looking. "But it must be Thursday," she insisted, going to the door to welcome the priest. "The *Staggerford Weekly* came out this morning."

"Well, what in the world . . . ?" murmured Agatha, puzzled, irritated, determined to put the man in his place. Say what you might about the shortcomings of this man's dear departed predecessor Father Finn—he was no intellectual giant and a bit on the timid side—but at least he knew the value of routine. As did Agatha.

"You don't live to be my age," she said to Father Healy as he crossed to her chair by the window, "without routine in your life."

"Pardon me?" he said, smiling and taking her hand. "I didn't catch that."

Oh dear, was she mumbling again? She called up her strongest voice to say, "Never mind, Father." She thought his smile the most attractive thing about him. And his voice was nicely modulated. He was said to deliver excellent homilies at Sunday Mass but Agatha couldn't attest to that, because she had been homebound since midwinter with lung disease resulting from congestive heart failure—or so said her doctor, who in her experience was correct only about half the time. She thought of her malady as merely a case of low-grade bronchitis resulting from the chilly air, because, although she was troubled by shortness of breath, she rarely coughed except when she stepped out into the cold.

Lillian called from the entryway, "Should I leave the door open, Agatha? It's getting warmer out."

"No, it's raining."

"But it's a warm rain."

"You know I hate the sound of it." This was about as long a sentence as she was able to utter in one breath. "Close the door and fetch Father a cup of tea."

Obediently Lillian shut out the rain and headed for the kitchen. Agatha addressed her on the way by. "Irishmen like it strong, remember, and use my good china."

Father Healy, strictly speaking, was not an Irishman. He was born of third-generation American parents (both of whom were only partially Irish) about seventy-five miles north of Staggerford in a town called Linden Falls, and he never drank tea if he could help it, but of course there was no helping it in the presence of Miss McGee. There seemed to be no possibility of adjusting this woman's preconceived notions.

"I'm sorry I didn't call ahead, Miss McGee, but since I was passing by . . ." He sat down in the wing chair facing her—his Saturday chair—and his expression turned serious. "Just before leaving the rectory, I got a phone call from a Mrs. Beverly Cooper who said you'd remember her. She was calling from the Thrifty Springs Motel and said—"

"I've never known anyone named Cooper."

"No, obviously—it's her married name. Twenty-five years ago her name was—let me see." He drew a slip of paper from his pocket. "Bingham."

Agatha gasped, "Beverly Bingham." She covered her eyes for fear of revealing emotion to her pastor.

"She's back in town to see you. We had quite a talk. She told me about your life together, what you did for her after the teacher was killed and her mother was put away. She says she hopes you don't harbor any hard feelings against her."

"Harbor" was the woman's word, a curiously old-fashioned expression, considering the lack of sophistication in her voice. The word was doubtless a relic from her time living in this stately old house with this old woman. And yet, thought Father Healy, Agatha wouldn't have been so old when the woman on the phone knew her. She'd have been in her fifties, scarcely any older than he himself was now. It was difficult for him to picture Miss McGee as anything but ancient. Even as a girl she must have been something of a prim old maid.

To keep her head from shaking she gripped her chin with a tremulous hand and turned away from Father Healy, gazing out at the wet gloom. A lifelong pillar of strength and reserve, Agatha was cursed these days with the shakes whenever strong emotion overtook her. So Beverly was back. Poor Beverly, the sweet daughter of a murdering mother. Beverly Bingham, who, having awakened in Agatha a maternal impulse that never went away, left town as Beverly Anderson, the wife of a soldier (she'd always had a weakness for uniforms), and traveled the world with him, sending out Christmas cards from as far away as Australia. And now she was back with a different last name.

"Cooper, you say? She's taken a second husband. Oh, the poor thing." She spoke with her eyes on the haze of rain falling into the river across the street. "She was famous for making poor choices." She paused for breath. "Beginning with her choice of parents."

"Yes, her mother killed people, she told me."

"Killed two men, she did . . . or three, if you count her husband . . . whom she put out of commission for the rest of his life. . . . Her husband, you see, was wrongfully thought to have killed the first man . . . a pots and pans salesman who came to their door . . . shot and killed at close range on their front porch. . . . Mr. Bingham, a native American, spent the rest of his life . . . in a penitentiary." She turned to face her pastor, her head bobbing like a toy on a spring. "Why did she call you? Why didn't she come directly to see me?"

"I have no idea, Miss McGee. She spoke of hard feelings— maybe she thinks you blame her for something; she didn't say."

"*My* hard feelings?"

"She didn't say whose."

"Nonsense." She fell silent. Father Healy saw her eyes shift inward, going over something in her past. Perhaps she nodded as well, though it may have been the tremor. His message delivered, he wanted to leave—he was on his way to the nearby village of Willoughby to oversee repairs to the church there, and then on to the city of Berrington, where he would have dinner with an old friend, a nurse in the hospital there named Libby Pearsall—but of course he must stay for the ink-black tea Lillian at length served him in a coffee mug. He thanked her, sipped, and burned his tongue.

The sight of the coffee mug brought Agatha out of her reverie. "Lillian, you don't listen . . . I said my good china."

When Lillian reached for the mug to rectify her error, the priest withheld it, and Agatha said, "Never mind." Lillian went back to her chair and pulled her garment-in-progress and her needles out of the plastic bag at her feet. Knitting, she listened to the two of them skate nimbly across the weather (spring was late this year and very wet) and the candidates in next month's school-board election, before they settled on the topic of St. James's Church in Willoughby. The repairs were proving more expensive than estimated, and Father Healy was particularly concerned, because St. James's was one of three churches in his care. Along with the local parish, St. Isidore's, he also served, due to the shortage of priests, Holy Spirit Church on the Sandhill Indian Reservation.

Priests weren't getting enough sex. That was Lillian's considered opinion concerning the Church's shortage of manpower. She must ask Father Healy sometime if this weren't true. It was a theory she hadn't been able to discuss with Agatha, because Agatha shied away from all topics having to do with human reproduction.

"I'm afraid St. Isidore's will have to carry St. James's for a while," the priest was saying. "We're down to our last penny in Willoughby."

"How dreadful," said Agatha.

She and her pastor were distracted from church repair by the increased tempo of clicking needles. Agatha gave him a long-suffering smile as she nodded across the room, where Lillian, finishing the shoulder of her garment and coming into several rows of plain stitches, had picked up speed as she tried and failed to remember a time in their long lives when Agatha uttered the word "sex."

"What are you knitting?" asked Father Healy.

"A sweater." Lillian's standard answer when she wasn't sure.

"Very colorful."

"Yes, Father." It was her favorite color, chartreuse. Pulling the entire piece out of the bag and smoothing it across her lap, she was shocked to discover how long and flat it was. It was a scarf. But if it was a scarf, why was there a shoulder in it? She quickly stuffed it back into her bag before Agatha noticed, before she was accused by Agatha of having a lazy brain.

"Well, I must be going," said Father Healy, finishing his tea. "I forgot to get the number of the motel for you. Sorry."

"Nonsense. We're perfectly able to look up telephone numbers, aren't we, Lillian."

"You bet." Lillian did the looking for both of them these days, having had her cataracts seen to recently. Agatha, though urged by Lillian and Janet Meers to have the same procedure done on herself, had put it off in favor of sitting in her chair and guessing who walked by and foregoing small print. Truth be told, she hadn't had much gumption for anything since her friend James O'Hannon died four years ago. Coming home from his funeral in Ireland, she was shocked to discover herself feeling dislocated in her home town. Effort spent on anything had seemed useless.

"I'll be back with Communion day after tomorrow," he told Agatha, smiling. "Eight-thirty again?"

"Eight-thirty is fine." She observed, not for the first time, that the man's eyes were nonjudgmental—surely a flaw in a priest of God.

"Good-bye, then."

"Good-bye, Father."

"How about you?" he asked Lillian as she handed him his coat. "Would you like to receive, too?"

She laughed. "Oh my, no. I'm not up that early."

"How about ten. I could come at ten."

"That's more like it. Except you don't know where I live."

"Not here?" He assumed these two elderly parishioners were housemates. An assumption that caused both women to laugh, for some reason.

Accompanying him across the wide front porch, Lillian explained, "I'm at Sunset Senior, just down the block from St. Isidore's.

I used to be neighbors to Agatha across the alley, but moved into Sunset last fall. My daughter Imogene's now living in my house, but she's trying to sell it. She wants one of them new apartments downtown. You know Imogene."

"No, I'm afraid . . ."

"Sure, everybody knows Imogene. She's the head muckety-muck over at the public library. She stood number two in her high school class, back in the days when there was real competition for grades."

About to dash to his car, he turned up his collar against the rain. "I'm afraid I haven't been to the library yet. I moved here just a month ago."

"Ask for Imogene when you go. She's a real firecracker."

"I'll do that. I'll see you Saturday at ten." He ran away.

Lillian laughed, calling after him, "Better be careful though, Father, she's looking for a man."

Driving away, he saw in his mirror a Lincoln town car pull up and park in his place.

Meanwhile, Agatha, going to the kitchen to make sure Lillian had turned out the fire under the teakettle, called to mind Beverly Bingham, who began ringing Agatha's doorbell when she was a schoolgirl. She needed to see Miles Pruitt, her English teacher, who was Agatha's lodger at the time. The first couple of visits she had a desperate look in her eyes, like someone who had waited until the very last moment to ask for help. Well, it was no wonder. The poor thing was living out in the gulch west of town with a mother absolutely out of her mind. After the tragedy—in November of her senior year—Agatha blamed all of Staggerford for what happened, herself no more nor less than her neighbors, and she still did. Everyone had known forever about Corrine Bingham's mental problems, but preferred not to think what it must have been like for the poor girl to live with that madwoman for eighteen years, to go home to the filthy chaos of that barnyard, that house, day after day.

It happened on a wet day, like today, shortly after noon. Corinne Bingham's mind snapped. Agatha was called away from her cup of tea at the Hub Cafe. This was when she was still teaching, so it must have been a Saturday; otherwise, what was she doing in the Hub at that hour? Anna Thea Workman, the high school principal's wife, drove her out to the gulch. Agatha had seen the Bingham farm only once before, almost fifty years earlier—think of it, living so long that you begin thinking in half-century segments!—when she accompanied her father on one of his campaign tours of western Berrington County. He was running for the state legislature. The place wasn't such a mess then, though it was spooky, being buried so deep in the ravine. Agatha didn't recall who lived there then. All she remembered was that it wasn't much past noon of a sunny autumn day and already the farmyard lay deep in shadow.

Returning to her chair by the window, Agatha was alarmed to see two strangers—a heavy, elderly woman and a tall man in a dark suit, perhaps her chauffeur—emerge from an enormously ostentatious automobile parked at the curb. Their faces hidden under two umbrellas, they came up her outer steps and her sloping sidewalk and proceeded slowly up to her front porch. Surely Lillian would know enough to fend them off. It was one thing to be on display as the ancient crone you were when your parish priest walked in; it was quite another to be discovered by strangers sitting here past noon in your robe and slippers without a smidgen of rouge on your chalky face.

But what did Lillian know! The screen door opened and in

came the strangers, the elderly woman making throaty, gurgling sounds, perhaps of pleasure, as she advanced upon Agatha with her hand out as though to be kissed. "Miss McGee, my dear, dear Miss McGee, we meet at last," she wheezed. "I've been meaning to make this pilgrimage since forever, but something always seems to come up. Well, once I heard you were under the weather I said to Leland here, I said, 'Bring the car around, Leland, we're driving to Staggerford this afternoon to see Miss McGee because . . .'" Here she paused to cough. "Because I need to tell her something very personal . . ." Overtaken by a paroxysm of coughing, she lowered herself into Lillian's chair. Lillian, heading once again for the kitchen, swerved past Agatha, uttering something she didn't quite catch. It sounded like "Dolly Squeaking."

The woman's companion, having paused in the entryway to remove his rubbers, looked vaguely familiar now as he sidled tentatively into the room. He was clearly of a different generation than the woman, surely no more than retirement age, not a great deal older than Father Healy, Agatha judged. "Pardon our intrusion, Miss McGee," he said in a voice familiar as well, but too far back in memory to retrieve. Standing at the stout woman's shoulder, and evidently seeing the puzzlement in Agatha's eyes, he added, helpfully, "We're the Edwardses from Rookery. My mother Lolly."

Why, of course. Lolly Edwards of KRKU radio (the Voice of Rookery) and longtime host of its morning call-in show, *Lolly Speaking*—not Dolly Squeaking. And this man Agatha took to be her chauffeur was actually her son Leland Edwards, ex-president of Rookery State College. As dean of the college, before he was raised to the presidency, Professor Edwards had called together a dozen retired teachers of sterling reputation, including Agatha, for the dedication of the new education building on campus. It was called the Simon P. Shea Teaching and Learning Center, and the highlight of the occasion for Agatha had been meeting Simon P.

Shea in the flesh. In 1950, the governor had proclaimed Professor Shea Minnesota's Teacher of the Half Century, and she had thought it a marvel that this man of such high standing was still around over thirty years later. He was eighty-something that year. And she thought it all the more miraculous that he should be able to stand up to the microphone and say witty and self-deprecating things to a hushed audience obviously in love with him.

When it was her turn to say a few words, this same audience fell silent again, but out of respect, not affection—Agatha's long years in the classroom had trained her to sense the difference and to expect no more. For most of her life she'd had respect from almost everyone who knew her—and thank God for that—but it was a lifelong puzzle to Agatha why this respect had so seldom evolved into something warmer, like love.

Lolly Edwards stopped coughing and said, "The respect you command is phenomenal, Miss McGee, and I've so looked forward to your calls over the years. I can just feel every ear in my listening audience perk up when you're on the air. In fact, it's gotten to be a joke around the station—when we run into a boring stretch, my station manager will say, 'Better call Staggerford and see what's on Miss McGee's mind.'"

"Oh, please! I'm long past the age (wheeze) when flattery means anything to me. Anyhow . . . I haven't phoned you more than five or six times in my life."

"Not often enough, that's true (cough), but a reliable, sensible voice over the years."

"Two years only."

"Oh come now. I remember many, *many* years ago speaking with you (cough, cough) about politics."

"If it was before two years ago, your memory is faulty, Mrs. Edwards. I distinctly recall my first conversation with you."

From her visitor came the same pitying look Agatha'd been

getting from certain other people who assumed she was senile. It was a look usually prompting her to react with an angry word, but this visitor was too distinguished to be treated like a common Staggerfordian. Besides, the poor woman's renewed fit of coughing left her no opening.

"I'll be right back with your oxygen," said her son, hurrying out the door.

Seeking distraction from the woman's deepening, engulfing cough—it came up through what sounded like a throatful of wet pebbles—Agatha called out, "Lillian!" and at that very moment Lillian, bless her, came into the room with a tray of tea things—cups, saucers, and plates of Belgian china that had been in Agatha's family for nearly a century. To make room for the tray on the coffee table, Lillian swept magazines and books onto the floor.

"This is my dear friend Lillian Kite," said Agatha, and Lolly Edwards acknowledged this introduction as best she could by turning her bleary eyes in Lillian's direction and giving her a benevolent nod.

Lillian advised, "What you need for that cough is a good shot of whiskey. My husband Lyle used to hack and spit till you'd swear he'd cough up his feet; then he'd have himself a shot of Old Crow and it'd quiet him right down. I'll be back in a jiffy."

"Oh, no," called Agatha, dismayed at the thought of Lillian rummaging through her meager liquor supply in the pantry and bringing out some dusty old bottle of congealed liqueur, but her friend was already gone through the swinging door into the kitchen. As Agatha feared, she returned with a ten-year-old bottle of sherry in one hand, an even older bottle of Cointreau in the other. "Agatha doesn't keep Old Crow on hand, but here's some sherry and some . . ." She examined the label. "Some Coin-true."

Professor Edwards returned, and while he untangled a long plastic tube and attached it to his mother's nose, Agatha considered going to her room and fixing herself up, but felt that Mrs. Edwards, in her condition, wouldn't stay long enough to make the effort worthwhile. Also, she wanted to be near the telephone when Beverly Bingham called.

Infused with oxygen and sherry-laced tea, however, Mrs. Edwards remained comfortably seated for half an hour or more, relating the news and gossip of Rookery as if Agatha and Lillian were interested. Professor Edwards, the dutiful son, having taken Father Healy's chair near the window, appeared to hang alertly on his mother's every word while keeping a watchful eye on the weather. Lillian, seated on a straight chair with a needlepoint seat, let her mind wander and was aware of scarcely a word being uttered.

At length, the woman inquired of Agatha whether she occupied this large old house alone.

"Oh no, Frederick Lopat, my nephew, lives here with me."

"And what does he do for a living?"

Agatha explained that Federick was a part-time rural mail carrier, and summers he was employed in the tourist industry.

"And what *exactly* does he do in the tourist industry?"

"He works in the tourist industry," Agatha repeated, pretending to be harder of hearing than she was, because she was ashamed to specify that her nephew posed as an Ojibwa Indian at the visitors' center beside U. S. Highway 71.

"We're both blessed in that way, Miss McGee. I of course couldn't continue on in my house in the college neighborhood if it weren't for Leland and his dear wife who occupy the upper floor." And here, for the first time, Agatha spied a crack in Mrs. Edwards's facade, a hitch in her delivery. "But his dear wife, I'm afraid, is dissatisfied (sob) with this arrangement."

"It's the trees, Mother."

"Oh, the trees," she said with disgust, dabbing at her eyes with a hankie. "Let's be on our way, Leland, before we embarrass ourselves."

Her son sprang to her side, a movement that aroused Lillian from her reverie, and he helped her to her feet, all the while explaining to Agatha that the north woods had a depressing effect on his wife, who was reared in North Dakota and thus not used to being surrounded by trees. With Leland wheeling her oxygen tank behind her, Lolly Edwards carried her broken spirit out the door without saying good-bye. She needed her son's support across the porch and down to their car.

Lillian gathered up the teacups.

"What was that all about?" mused Agatha, under her breath. Watching them depart beneath their two umbrellas, she sorted through what she'd been told by Mrs. Edwards over the past half hour and determined that none of it had been of an urgent or personal nature. Obviously Mrs. Edwards forgot her reason for the visit. "And how did she know I was under the weather?"

After the car had pulled away from the curb, Agatha got to her feet again and, carrying her two bottles of liqueur, tottered into the kitchen behind Lillian. She had half a mind to ask Lillian if she'd been spreading it around about Dr. Hammond's diagnosis of congestive heart failure, but she held her tongue because Lillian, of all people, had been acting testy lately. She returned to her chair, and as the sky became darker and the rain came down heavier, she dozed off.

She was awakened by the opening and closing of the back door—Frederick coming in from Kruger's pool hall where he spent most of his winter afternoons—and the grinding gears of a dump truck spilling out an enormous pile of sandbags across her boulevard. After speaking for a minute with Lillian in the kitchen, Frederick came through the dining room and moved stealthily across the living room toward the stairway. He wore a faded blue baseball cap pulled low over his haunted blue eyes. A length of skin was exposed beyond the cuffs of his faded denim jacket.

"Hello, Frederick."

He stopped abruptly and turned to Agatha with a worried expression. "Sorry." He removed his cap and stood at attention.

"For what, pray tell? You didn't wake me."

"Good."

"Frederick, would you please go out there and tell that man I don't want . . . that unsightly pile on my grass?"

He went out and chatted for a minute in the rain with the truck driver, a man he knew from the pool hall, and returned to report that the next load would go on a neighbor's boulevard.

"What's it like outside?"

"Warm."

"Frederick, I had a curious visit this afternoon from Lolly Edwards."

"Oh?"

"You know who I mean. From Rookery?"

"Yep."

"Well, she came to tell me something personal, she said, and then . . . she left without saying what it was. The poor woman obviously suffers from a lazy brain."

"Huh."

It was to conceal the laziness of his own brain from his Aunt Agatha that Frederick, whenever possible, spoke to her only in monosyllables. She'd quit trying to open him up. For a time after he came to live here, they had a contest of wills and that was when she discovered how stubborn he could be, how deeply buried were his feelings.

"Is that the *Weekly*?" she asked, pointing to the newspaper under his arm.

"Yep." He showed her the headline BADBATTLE TO FLOOD!!!

"Nonsense," she said. "I've heard that before."

He then creased the paper open to page two and pointed to a small headline under the obituaries. Before she could read it the telephone rang. Although it was within easy reach, she waited for Frederick to pick it up because if it were some burglar or rapist with Agatha in mind she liked to have it known that there was a man in the house.

"Yep," he said into the phone and handed it to her.

"Beverly, my gracious," said Agatha.

"I'm so embarrassed, Miss McGee." It was not Beverly, but Lolly Edwards not sounding embarrassed in the least. "I came away from your lovely house without saying why I'd come. I tell you I'm in danger of forgetting my own name these days."

"And your message is?" prompted Agatha, eager to free the phone for Beverly's call.

"My message is this, my dear, that you simply must hold your memorial service before you pass on."

"My memorial service! . . . Goodness, that's the least of my worries." Surely Mrs. Edwards had gone off the deep end.

"I know it sounds ridiculous, Miss McGee, but I did it myself years ago, and it was downright wonderful. You get to hear yourself praised instead of waiting until it's too late. I mean I was on death's doorstep, and by the time it was over I felt like I was nineteen. I've been operating on the residuals ever since."

"Where are you calling from? Are you home already?"

"Oh my, no (a laugh, a cough), I'm calling from our car. Now listen, Miss McGee, with your scads of former students all over America, you're going to be absolutely knocked out by the tributes they pay you. You're going to feel like you're nineteen again. I guarantee it."

"Who'd want to be nineteen?"

"I know, you have to take it on faith, but with your reputation, you'll get more over-the-top eulogies than anyone else in KRKU's listening area, and my engineer and I will be more than happy to come and do a remote from Staggerford. (Cough, cough.) Just think of it, my dear, your praises sung over the airwaves. Take it from me, I was on death's doorstep, so that Leland had to practically carry me into the service and I walked out a new woman. Been healthy as an ox ever since." A statement belied by a renewed fit of coughing, which doubtless didn't permit her to hear Agatha sign off:

"Thank you so much for calling and good-bye."

Putting down the phone, she found that Frederick had been replaced at her side by Lillian. "Good-bye, Agatha, the dishes are washed and put away. I'll see you tomorrow."

"Tell me the truth, Lillian. Have you been spreading it around about my illness?"

"Not a word."

"Well, somebody's talking. Otherwise, how did Lolly Edwards know I'm not up to par?"

Lillian shrugged. "Somebody must've called into her program about you."

This possibility made Agatha shiver. "What do you say when people ask after my health?"

"What you told me to say—'She's the same.'" Fuming, Lillian slipped into her chartreuse nylon windbreaker, hung her purse over her arm, and picked up her knitting. A stoical companion all her life, Lillian's fuse was growing shorter with age. She resented being doubted by Agatha, who couldn't seem to take her faithful ways for granted. Agatha was about to say how upset this made her, having her privacy invaded like this, but before she got it out, Lillian said good-bye and pulled the door shut behind her.

Well! Walking out in the middle of a conversation—how insulting! And before Agatha had a chance to point out that serving

tea in a coffee mug and knitting a shoulder in a scarf were two certain signs of a lazy brain.

She picked up the *Weekly* and looked at the article Frederick
left with her. ESTEEMED CITIZEN IN DECLINING HEALTH. "My Lord,"
she exclaimed aloud, holding the paper up close to her eyes, reading the article through, squinting and mumbling and solving the
mystery of how Lolly Edwards knew of her illness.

"Frederick," she called, and when he appeared on the stairway,
she said, speaking of the *Weekly*'s editor, "Lee Fremling, like his father before him, is said to drink too much."

Frederick nodded his agreement, having seen the man in his
cups.

Pointing to the article, she continued, "But it's partly my own
fault of course . . . for moping around the house all day. Get out
the car tomorrow, Frederick; we'll go downtown. We'll start at the
Weekly office and go grocery shopping . . . and pick up a prescrip-
tion at the drug store. I need to be seen out and about."

FRIDAY

Agatha slipped into her bright green raincoat, stepped out her back door for the first time in sixty days, and unfurled her umbrella against the thin drizzle that had been falling all night. The chilly morning air caused her to wheeze as she made her way, on Frederick's arm and between the soggy low spots in her yard, to his ancient Oldsmobile idling noisily in the alley.

"Will the rain never stop, Frederick?"

"Yep."

"When?"

"Maybe tomorrow," he said, putting two words together for a change.

As he was helping her into the passenger side, Lillian Kite's daughter, Imogene, stepped out her back door across the alley, strode over to the Oldsmobile, and got into the back seat. Her new spring coat of wine-colored poplin featured epaulets and a double row of brass buttons.

Irked, as always, by the woman's presumption and forwardness, Agatha asked in a high, sugary voice, "Would you like a ride to work, Imogene?"

"Don't mind if I do," was the acidic reply.

Frederick got in and they headed downtown. "Engine's cold," he explained when it died along River Street. He patted the dashboard fondly, as if to encourage the car to do better.

Which it did, and as they turned onto Coolidge Avenue, Agatha, doing her best to be civil, asked Imogene, "Have you had any nibbles on your house?"

"Doesn't matter," she answered evasively. "I bought a whole slew of flood insurance, so after the water goes down I can walk away from the place."

"Don't be silly. We've never had a flood on River Street."

"Oh yeah? In the flood of eighty-six practically the whole town was under water."

"Eighty-six?" Agatha squinted into the past. "We had no flood in eighty-six."

"*Eighteen* eighty-six . . ." Under her breath, under the noise of the engine, Imogene added, ". . . smarty pants."

Crossing the Coolidge Avenue Bridge, Agatha was stunned by the sight of water lapping at the foundation of the old brewery. After Karlstad Beer went bankrupt in 1932, this imposing and useless building of brick and broken windows housed a couple of other ill-fated businesses before it was finally abandoned to hoboes during the Depression and to rats and bats thereafter.

"I heard my father speak of high water sixty years ago," she told Frederick, who had pulled over onto the apron of the bridge. Despite the care he had given his old car, it bucked and rattled in neutral as traffic sped past them. "It was my first year away at college," she continued. "He said the brewery was inundated. But I've never known the water to rise this high since then. And see there!" she exclaimed, pointing upstream at what looked like an army of people milling about at the edge of the Hemlock Addition. They appeared to be walking and standing on white linen pillows. "What are they doing, Frederick?"

"Sandbagging."

"Why there, for goodness sake? Surely that's no lower ground than River Street."

"Hemlock Drive is nine feet lower than River Street in places," offered Imogene from her bottomless fund of factual knowledge.

"Well then, why do I have a truckload of sandbags in my front yard?" she asked.

Imogene contended, "Because we have the mayor living among us."

Agatha, because Mayor Thaddeus Druppers was a friend of hers, turned and gave her neighbor a withering look.

Imogene, a long-faced woman of large masculine features and ghostlike paleness, returned Agatha's expression with her most defiant glare and said, "Well, it's true, Agatha. Ever since Ted and Nellie Druppers moved to our neighborhood, the snowplows and street repair crews always start their work on River Street."

"If what you say is factual, Imogene, I'm sure it's out of respect for Mayor Druppers . . . and not something he himself requested." Agatha forestalled further argument by smiling and complimenting her passenger on her new coat. It was a trick she learned long ago and it shut the woman up every time, because she couldn't handle kindness.

Agatha turned to face front as Frederick shifted gears and proceeded slowly along Coolidge. "And I don't know when I've ever seen your hair looking so nice," she added, laying it on thick. "Who does your hair, if I may ask?"

Imogene, directing her gaze out her side window, muttered, "Shear Perfection, over on Second." It was the last thing she said before getting out and climbing the steps to her library.

The *Weekly* had been published in the same storefront building on Main Street, between the movie theater and Barker's Appliance and Bottlegas, since before Agatha was born. When the editor's mother and grandmother were alive, the place used to have a tidy appearance, but now it was a dingy mess. The paper itself used to be more interesting, too, in Agatha's opinion, with fewer typos and more substantial news. This was because Lee Fremling's father, the editor before him (and the original heavy drinker in the family), had a wife and a mother to guide him. Poor Lee, who was married only briefly at the age of nineteen, had no one to keep him on the straight and narrow. He appeared to be the same heavy, sparkless, sloe-eyed boy he was in high school thirty years ago. Agatha regretted never having had him as a student; surely she'd have been able to light a fire under him. She'd spent her entire career in the now defunct Catholic elementary. The Fremlings had been staunchly Lutheran.

Watching him rise from his desk and come forward to greet her, Agatha had a hard time believing that Lee was staunchly anything nowadays. He was a fat, shambling, smiling creature, bewhiskered and poorly dressed. "Hi," he simply said, not even addressing her by name.

She took for a brief moment the soft, moist hand he offered her and said, "I've come to register a complaint, Mr. Fremling."

"Hi, French," he interrupted, using the boyhood nickname Frederick still went by at Kruger's pool hall.

"Did you hear me, Mr. Fremling? I'm here . . . to ask what right you have to publicize the state of my health . . . for all the world to see."

"What?" he said, a vague look coming into his eyes. His short-sleeved knit golf shirt, she noticed, was a size too small and frayed at the collar.

"Page two of this week's edition . . . the article about my visit to the doctor."

No change came over his stupidly slack expression, except that his smile began to fade. He shrugged and said, "One of my reporters."

Suppressing the temptation to take him by the ear and give his head a rough shake, she asked, "Do you mean you are unaware of what appears in your paper?"

"The news I leave to the news staff."

"But you read it before it goes in . . . that's an editor's responsibility."

"Oh, I'm not editor anymore."

"You most certainly are!"

She caught him smiling and rolling his eyes at Frederick. She wondered, Could I be wrong? She had never in her life known anyone but a Fremling to edit the *Staggerford Weekly*.

Fremling picked up a current issue, turned to page two, and read, his expression growing serious. "Sorry you're sick," he said, folding the paper. "Lung disease and a bad heart. Bummer." He noticed the illness in her eyes now—a downsizing of the woman's ego, a bleary look, a vulnerability that no one had ever seen there before. Two thoughts crossed his mind. It occured to him to wonder who would take her place as Staggerford's queen mother and, second, whether anyone on his staff knew her well enough to write her obituary. "My grandma had heart failure. Died of it."

"Mr. Fremling, who is editing the *Weekly* if you're not?"

"Leslie Hokanson."

An unfamiliar name in town. "Does he come from Rookery? There are Hokansons in Rookery."

"Les!" he called, and a young woman's voice answered from behind a partition, "Yeah, whatcha want?"

"Come on up front a minute, would you?"

"Hold your horses, I'm on the phone."

"She'll be just a minute. She's on the phone."

Agatha, taking Frederick's arm, turned to leave. Fremling accompanied them to the door.

"If she is the editor, Mr. Fremling, what are you?"

"Publisher."

"I see. And as publisher, what do you do?"

"I oversee three newpapers. I've bought the *Loomis Messenger* and the *Stabler World*."

"Oh my, a press baron," she said, a glimmer of something lively coming into her eyes, the hint of a smile on her wrinkled lips. "Your readers will thank you for not sticking your nose into their private lives. Good-bye, Mr. Fremling."

Holding the door for them, he said, "G'bye, Miss McGee. So long, French."

On their way down the street and around the corner to the grocer's, Agatha said, "If I didn't know better . . . I'd take the newspaper office for a front."

"A front?" inquired Frederick, puzzled.

"A front for some illegal operation . . . drugs, say, or counterfeiters."

He chuckled.

"Well, didn't you notice . . . the empty area at the back? Where's his press? Where's his linotype machine?"

Frederick shrugged rather than jolt her with the fact that for the past ten years the *Weekly* had been printed in Loomis, that linotype was long outmoded, computers having taken its place. These days, change of any kind was bad news to Agatha.

It was the same in Druppers' Grocery, where the owner, seventy-five-year-old Thaddeus Druppers, was seldom on duty anymore. Finding a stranger behind the meat counter, Agatha refused to place her order until he revealed his name and assured her of his qualifications as a butcher. "Three years in the army, Ma'am, as a meatcutter for Uncle Sam."

"All right then, two of your very leanest pork chops."

He showed her several chops before she approved; then she turned to inspect the items Frederick had gathered together in a basket.

"Cake mix? Tomato soup? Frederick . . . we don't *need* any of these things. What's gotten into you?"

He showed her the list she gave him. That it corresponded to everything in the basket and yet was obviously written in her hand puzzled her for a moment, before she realized it was an old list.

"Put everything back!" The shrillness of her voice startled the butcher who quickly wrapped the chops and retreated into his walk-in cooler. Frederick, wise enough to know that her anger, though directed at him, was actually frustration at her own carelessness, obediently retraced his route through the store, emptying the basket.

"You'll have to come back with today's list," she said, meeting him at the checkout counter.

"This afternoon," he agreed.

The checker, too, was a stranger, a middle-aged woman with dyed blond hair and—of all things—sunglasses. Agatha, abiding by a lifelong policy against speaking to anyone whose eyes she could not look into, didn't inquire about her identity until the woman, handing her her change, surprised her by saying, "Thank you, Miss McGee."

It took her a moment to place the woman's voice and attach a name to it. "You're one of the Raft girls. Are you Karen Raft?"

"No, I'm LeeAnn."

"LeeAnn—but I thought you lived in Texas." Agatha's connection with the hardscrabble Raft family had been through LeeAnn's sister Janet Meers, whose son and daughter were Agatha's godchildren.

"Right, Miss McGee, I did live in Texas. I was married to a whacko from Waco till I divorced him and moved to L.A. for a while, and now I'm back home. The paper says you been sick. Are you okay again now?"

"Except for spells of dementia. We came downtown with the wrong grocery list. You remember my nephew, Frederick, do you?"

"Sure, we been havin' a few beers down at Kruger's together. Hi, French." She winked at him.

"Hi," said Frederick, looking at his shoes and blushing.

"I'm livin' out on the farm with Dad. I guess I'm just a farm-girl at heart."

"And how *is* your father?" Agatha asked.

"Not so hot. Emphysema, you know, from smoking all his life."

"And Stephen?" Agatha's godson was away at college. "Has he been home lately?"

"Stephen's home now. He's helping sandbag round their place. Its road's real low out where they live, you know, right near the water."

Agatha pictured the road along a pretty forested bend of the Badbattle northeast of town, leading to the enormous house high over the river where Janet and her husband, Randy Meers, a realtor, had reared two children, Stephen and Sara. Or rather, Janet had reared them. Randy was an unreliable husband and father. He was off somewhere tending to his parents' real estate business, it seemed, whenever a crisis arose. Agatha recalled his being gone during the blizzard of 1987, and again when Stephen fell out of a tree and broke his arm. He even disappeared the day Janet gave birth to Sara. Agatha considered Janet, now in her early forties, one of her two closest friends—the other, of course, being Lillian.

"Where is Randy?" she asked. With the river lapping at their foundation, it was safe to say he was gone again.

"Jeez, I don't know, Miss McGee. I guess Rookery. Since his dad put him in charge of their Rookery office he's hardly ever home."

Frederick, eager to leave, picked up their package of meat and headed for the door, with LeeAnn calling after him, "Hey, French, you gonna be at Kruger's later? I heard they got a bunch of new tunes on the jukebox."

He turned and gave her a brief little smile and a shrug.

Agatha had planned to go next to Phil's Pharmacy for a refill of her Lanoxin tablets, and then to Ace Hardware for a new extension cord for her living room floor lamp, but she felt suddenly weak in the knees. Sending Frederick on these errands, she collapsed, exhausted, into the passenger seat of the Oldsmobile. It was a measure of her fatigue that when she saw Lillian walking along the sidewalk in her typically distracted frame of mind—perhaps imagining her next chartreuse knitting project—she did not even roll down her window and call to her.

If it were anyone else staying at the Thrifty Springs Motel, she'd have called off the visit in favor of a nap, but her curiosity was too great concerning Beverly Cooper. Once the premier motel along Highway 71, the Thrifty Springs had gone to seed. Caught up in the optimism of the early sixties, the owners built it a mile and a half from town, expecting Staggerford to expand in that direction. Years later, it was still a mile and a half from town standing forlornly on a windswept hill, its paint peeling, its perpetual VACANCY sign hanging crooked in the rain.

While Frederick was in the office inquiring after Beverly Cooper, Agatha watched a woman and a girl carrying boxes from a large blue van into the endmost room. It was the vehicle's garish robin's-egg shade of blue that stirred her memory. Janet Meers drove a van as big and bright as that, the only one of its kind in town. When Frederick returned, she asked him to drive ahead for a closer look. Goodness, it *was* Janet Meers.

She lowered her window. "Janet, what are you doing here?"

"Agatha!" Janet's eyes, under the hood of her raincoat, registered both joy and concern. "What are *you* doing here?"

"I'm here to visit a guest in the motel." She tried to see past the open door of the endmost room. "Is that Stephen in there? I'm told he's come home to help you . . ." She was tempted to use the noun "sandbag" as a verb, the way everyone else was doing these days, but decided against it. "To defend your house against the flood."

Janet laughed. "Boy, you sure don't waste any time finding stuff out. He just got in last night."

"I saw LeeAnn at Druppers'."

A shift in the wind blew rain in Agatha's face, and Janet got into the back seat and closed the door. "Hi, Fredriko."

Looking straight ahead, he nodded and said, "Janet."

"She said your house was in danger," Agatha continued, cranking her window shut.

"If not the house, the road to it. They figure we could be stranded. That's why we're moving in here for a few days."

"But why this godforsaken place? You could have gone at least to the Holiday Inn."

"Because it's ours."

"Yours?" She turned to look at Janet—the wide-set intelligent eyes, the ruddy complexion, the rain glistening in her dark hair. Agatha remembered snowflakes in her hair the night she came in from the country to stay at Agatha's house because the roads were filling up with snow and she was about to give birth. And now the baby—Stephen—was twenty. Goodness, where does time go?

"Randy bought the place on speculation last summer," Janet explained. "I tell him we ought to change the name to the White Elephant Motel."

"But I thought Randy was smarter than that." Or so Janet

claimed. Having known Randy from the time he was twelve, Agatha had seen no evidence of it.

"He bought it on his parents' advice. Can you believe it, Agatha? They're both in their late seventies and they're still calling the shots in that business. They've lost their good judgment."

"Well, if it's yours on speculation, where's your FOR SALE sign? Summers everybody and his brother passes by here."

"A FOR SALE sign on a motel kills business. We've taken out ads in the trade journals."

"Janet, load up your boxes and come stay at my house."

"Oh, we couldn't do that."

"But you must."

"We'd disturb your peace, both of you. Sara's on the telephone night and day with her friends."

"Nonsense. Frederick will be glad of the company. Am I right, Frederick? After all these years of living with an old spook like me."

Frederick, staring out at the rain, chuckled softly.

"For my own peace of mind, Janet. I can't think of you holed up in this dreary place."

After a moment of silence, looking the Thrifty Springs over, Janet sighed, "Yes, isn't it the pits?"

Sara, a petite, dark-haired beauty, seventeen years old, appeared in the doorway of the room, a cell phone to her ear.

"Frederick, help them with their boxes, would you?"

"Never mind, Fredriko, we've only got two or three. We'll put them in the van and follow you."

"But before you do," said Agatha, "there's somebody here I want you to meet. . . . You remember my telling you about Beverly Bingham, surely."

"Beverly Bingham? She's here?"

"Nope, she isn't," said Frederick.

Agatha shot him a stern look. "I beg your pardon?"

He nodded. "She's gone."

"She can't be gone."

"They said in the office."

"She's gone?"

"Checked out last night."

Janet, at Agatha's insistence, summoned Stephen into town for lunch. He was a large, smiley, long-haired young man who drove up in a black Trans Am and entered the house energized by his work in holding off the impending flood. His talk was so loud and relentless that he seemed to Frederick—sitting across the table from him and nibbling on a sandwich—to be using up all the oxygen in the room.

"There's a civil engineer working with us and he says last year there was almost as much spring runoff as this year, but what kept the river from flooding was the hard frost we got every night—it kept the river frozen, so it thawed only a little at a time, but the trouble this year is that once it got warm it stayed warm and all the snow melted all at once. Plus all the rain. Hey, Agatha, this is great soup—what kind is it?"

"Campbell's chicken noodle, straight out of the can. The greatness you speak of . . . is in your hunger, I assure you. Not in the soup."

"No, it's great, I mean it. Hey, Mom, whatcha got against canned soup? How come we hafta have homemade all the time."

"I'll tell you the reason," said Agatha, answering for Janet. "It's that I never learned to cook." As usual, whenever this handsome, good-natured, nimble young man came to call, Agatha felt her spirit rise; her heart grew light; she felt playful. Even her breathing seemed to improve.

Stephen finished his soup and moved on to his sandwich. "So

anyhow, this civil engineer—his name is Harry and he's up here from the Cities—he brought a sandbagging crew out along our road this morning, and he said if it stays this warm we're in for trouble, except he didn't say 'trouble,' he said 'disaster.'"

"Oh dear," said Janet, "they're predicting highs in the sixties for this weekend."

"Harry says if it floods it'll hit Willoughby first, 'cuz that's the first town after the Badbattle comes out of the deep woods, and whatever happens in Willoughby will happen here in Staggerford a day or so later. He says it could happen that everybody's house along the riverbed will be under water."

Agatha caught Janet shooting her an anxious look and responded with a shrug.

"So I said to Harry, what're we doin' out here in the country; we better start sandbaggin' in town, and he says Staggerford's too spread out for sandbaggin' to do much good, 'cept right out here along your stretch of river, Agatha. He says out here's where we go to work tomorrow, right outside your living room window."

Having wolfed down his sandwich, Stephen got up to leave, gave Agatha and his mother a peck on the cheek, ignored his sister, and nodded good-bye to Frederick.

"So look out your window tomorrow," he told Agatha. "I'll be wavin' atcha."

Frederick lingered at the table after the others had left the kitchen. He sipped his third and fourth cup of cooling coffee and thought that it was too bad, for Agatha's sake, that he himself didn't have more of Stephen's opinionated talkativeness. With his gift of gab, Stephen would go places, amount to something. Frederick had noticed how certain people made Agatha's eyes light up as soon as they stepped foot in the door, and Stephen was one of them. His mother, Janet, was another. The parish priest, too. Not Lillian, he was sorry to say. Nor himself, and more's the pity.

He remembered how hard it was to live in this house at first, what with Agatha always trying to get him to speak up, day in, day out, always hoping he'd come up with something interesting to say. About all he ever heard down at the pool hall was who was shacking up with who—not the kind of thing you talked about in this house—and how much water all the old fellows had in their rain gauges every morning. It got so bad that he was about ready to find another room somewhere and move out, but he never got around to it; and then after a few months Agatha let up on him, and they'd been getting along pretty well ever since.

Of course it wasn't as relaxing as living in the Morgan Hotel, which he did when he first came home from the army. Agatha did tend to keep him always on edge a little bit—about keeping his room picked up, keeping his car clean, keeping the snow shoveled, keeping the grass cut, and going to mass every Sunday besides. But the older he got—he'd be fifty-two in August—the more he saw that the pros of living there far outweighed the cons. For one thing his room at the Morgan Hotel was cold from September to May and hotter than blazes all summer, whereas here Agatha kept the thermostat pushed way up all winter and she had all these big old shade trees round the house that acted like an air conditioner in the summer. Besides, the Morgan was history—bulldozed down to make a parking lot.

For another thing—and this came as a suprise to him—he rather enjoyed all the people coming around here to visit. At the Morgan he never saw anybody up close enough to talk to, except Grover, the desk clerk, from one week to the next, which was all right with Frederick—he was Mr. Shy in those days. But those days were long gone. Not that he had all that much to say even now, but it was fun to listen to what other folks had to say. He wished he'd been here yesterday and seen Lolly Edwards. There was a woman bartender down at the pool hall named Millicent Pease who hadn't missed *Lolly Speaking* on the radio for something like four years running, and Frederick would have dearly loved to be able to tell her he saw Lolly in person.

Lillian arrived after lunch. It had been years since she missed an afternoon at Agatha's house. As one who naturally drifted toward the rote and familiar aspects of life, Lillian formed this habit as Agatha's neighbor and carried it into her old age. Neither of them was quite aware of how much Agatha depended on Lillian's help around the house. While Janet and Sara settled into their room upstairs, Lillian looked up the number of Thrifty Springs, then dialed the phone and handed it to Agatha.

From her many questions, Agatha learned only that a woman named Beverly Cooper and a man checked in yesterday for two or possibly three nights and abruptly checked out this morning. The woman looked forty-five, maybe fifty; the man seemed quite a bit younger. Did the woman seem agitated? Who was the man? Where were they on their way to? The desk clerk, refusing to speculate, was no help.

Deflated, she hung up and watched Lillian knitting for a time; then she was distracted by a car moving slowly along the street with at least three men inside, looking at the river. She knew by the insignia on the door (the head of a stag) that it was an official city car. "What do you think, Lillian, will we concern ourselves with the flood?"

Her friend, concentrating on her garment-in-progress, mumbled affirmatively, negatively, or indecisively—it was impossible to tell which.

"I'm inclined to trust history," Agatha went on. "History tells me that only once in my lifetime has the Badbattle overflowed its banks. I was away at college. My father reported that a little water trickled into the basement. Which was extraordinary because this is the highest property along River Street."

Lillian, placidly knitting, said, "Thaddeus Druppers claims it's going to be the flood of the century."

"Who?"

"Thaddeus Druppers, in the store."

"But he's never *in* the store anymore."

Lilllian sensed another of Agatha's trivial arguments coming on. For most of her life, Lillian had always given in, because she disliked arguing, and because Agatha was usually right. But now that her patience was wearing thin and Agatha was wrong about half the time, she'd begun challenging her old friend. "He was in the store this morning. Oh, yes, I saw him there."

"I was there this morning myself, Lillian . . ." She paused to gather oxygen and strength, and just as she was about to press her point, the phone rang.

"Agatha, I see by the paper you're under the weather." A woman's voice.

"It's a scandal what they put in the paper these days. Who is this?"

"Dort."

"Oh, Dort. There's a flood coming your way. Have you heard?" Covering the mouthpiece she leaned toward Lillian. "It's Dort Holister, in Willoughby." The Holister sisters, Dort and Calista, together with their brother, Howard, operated the Willoughby post office.

"We've already got some roads under water out here," said Dort. "I'm calling to tell Frederick to stay home tomorrow. He'd need a boat to get around his route."

"I'll tell him. . . . How is Calista?"

"Oh, the poor thing; she suffers."

"Is it shingles again?"

"No, arthritis. It's always bad in the damp. Here, I'll put her on."

Dort's sister came on the line with a timid, "Agatha?"

"Calista, I was just telling Dort there's a flood coming your way."

"Yes, so we're told."

"I think the two of you should come in and stay with me till it's over."

"Oh, that would be up to Dort."

The line fell silent while the sisters held a consultation.

"No, Agatha, Dort says thanks a million, but there's no need."

"I've got two empty bedrooms upstairs."

"Dort says we're not in danger." She added with a touch of pride in her voice, "We occupy the highest street in Willoughby, you know."

"Of course I know, but is it high enough? is what I'm wondering."

"Thanks a million, but you know Dort." By which, Agatha knew, she meant strong-minded. Able-bodied for her age. Always correct in her judgments. "It's nice talking to you, Agatha; thanks for calling."

"I didn't call you. Dort called me."

"Here, I'll put her back on. Oh, say, we saw it in the paper about your health. How are you?"

"Never better!" Which, for the moment, was true. A surge of anger had made her suddenly feel young and vigorous. "That item had no business being in the paper. And to prove it, Frederick and I will come visit you this afternoon."

"Oh, goody, I'll bake a pie."

What had she done? she asked herself after hanging up the phone. She caused herself a heap of trouble was what she'd done. She had to send Lillian home, she had to summon Frederick from the pool hall, and she had to fix herself up for the Holisters. She simply *must* stop being so impulsive.

· · ·

Left and right on their way to Willoughby they saw inundated fields and water lapping at the shoulders of the highway. And still it rained.

"Will we turn around now?" suggested Agatha, convinced at last that the flood was at hand. "We can't spend the night stuck in the post office."

"No, we got a few hours leeway."

"How do you know? . . . It's practically over the road."

"The flatness," he declared, gesturing at the level land left and right. "It isn't like at home, in a valley."

"We'd better turn around, Frederick."

"There it is," he said, nodding ahead at the village, the American flag flying over the hilltop post office. One of Willoughby's few streets was indeed under water, but Main Street, which ran over the crest of the hill, was high and dry.

They parked in the alley, in order to enter the living quarters at the back of the post office. Climbing the three steps to the stoop, Agatha predicted, "A half hour at the most," but Frederick knew better. The Holisters, all three of them, clung to visitors like prisoners. Even Frederick, whom they saw every Saturday, had to pry himself loose after he sorted his mail and was thus often late getting to his route.

Dort Holister, who'd been watching for them with her one good eye, threw open the door and took Agatha in her arms. "Oh, dearie, we're so honored to have you come see us. Everybody's talking about how sick you are. Come in, come in. Don't you get tired of this dreary weather? Doesn't it seem like we haven't seen sunshine since last fall?" Dort was a large, loud woman, neatly dressed in a style of twenty years ago—a gray gabardine pantsuit, a white blouse with a starched collar standing up around her neck. Having lost her left eye to cancer several years ago, she wore glasses with a frosted lens. Evident in her ruddy complexion was a case of hypertension. She was Willoughby's postmistress.

Calista, a paler version of her sister, came limping in from another room and gave Agatha a tight but silent embrace. Both women had been friends of Agatha's for nearly half a century, having passed through her sixth grade, a year apart, before World War II.

"Calista," said Agatha. "Give it to me straight—how are you?"

"Oh, arthritis and such."

"Arthritis has been a plague on the Holister house for generations," said Dort. "Howie has it. Our mother had it."

"Dort has it but never complains," said her sister.

"Oh, tut, a hitch in my wrist now and then is all." Dort led them to their dining table. "Sit down both of you. Howie will be in in a minute, Frederick; he's out front, sweeping."

The sisters, less than a year apart in age, looked so much alike, thought Frederick, that Dort's frosted lens used to be his only way of telling them apart. But now, seeing them once a week as part-time postman, he'd begun to notice subtler differences in their coloring and in their manner of speaking. Calista was the quiet one, deferring to her effusive sister and her cantankerous brother in most things.

"Now what will you two have to drink?" Dort wanted to know. "Coffee, tea, or fruit punch?"

"Or a Bloody Mary?" said Calista uncertainly. "I'm sometimes fond of a Bloody Mary along about this time in the afternoon."

Were it the sisters alone, Agatha would have accepted a Bloody Mary—she'd had one here a time or two before and found it bracing—but of course one had one's dignity to uphold in the presence of Frederick and Howard. She asked for tea. Frederick, though dying for his beer at this time of the afternoon, would have the fruit punch. He knew that because he was driving, his Aunt Agatha wouldn't allow him alcohol.

The Holisters handled fewer pieces of mail here than almost any other post office in the Midwest, and yet their current congressman, Dale Lindquist, had been able to keep the place open for the good of Willoughby, which, before having lost the railroad and its high school, used to be considerably larger. It was said that losing the post office, too, would wipe out the town entirely. Congressman Lindquist had let it be known that it was safe only until the death of the current postmistress. Agatha realized what a strain it was for Dort, two years beyond retirement age, to hold the future of Willoughby in her arthritic hands.

"It's got so Dort can't sort mail anymore, her hands are that crippled up," said Calista, taking the chair with her back to the window because the light hurt her eyes. "Howie has to do all the sorting these days, and Howie hates sorting."

Because this was more of their personal lives than Dort would care to admit, Agatha expected her to change the subject. Which she did. "I don't know what's taking Howie so long, Frederick; usually he's done cleaning up by this time."

"Probably talking to somebody come in to check their mailbox," said Calista.

Dort raised a finger for silence. No voices from beyond the door to the business end of the building. Only the sound of rain lashing the windows. "I'm sure he won't be long, Frederick, or you can step through there and see him."

"No, no, that's okay." Frederick found it amusing the way the Holisters assumed that he was fond of Howie. Nobody was fond of Howie—didn't they know that?

Settled around the table, they took up the flood. Dort said that half of Willoughby was evacuated, but she herself, despite a nightmare Calista had had the other night, was confident that the post office was high enough to be spared.

"I've been having the craziest dreams," Calista verified.

"I always forget my dreams the minute I wake up," said Agatha.

"I'll sometimes remember the tail end," said Dort.

They looked to Frederick—it was his turn—but he had nothing to add.

Calista said, "I dream so much about dead people all the time."

"About the only dream I remember lately," said Agatha, "I was down in the cellar in my laundry room with a whole pile of dirty clothes . . . and the washer went on the blink."

"We've got so careless, we don't care what day we wash," said Dort.

"The last dead one I dreamed of was Mother," said Calista. "Just the other night."

"I wash every Monday," said Agatha.

Calista went on: "I didn't tell you, Dort, but there she was, plain as day, in the parlor darning socks, and there was a mouse going across the room kind of crooked and slow, and she took aim and pitched her old wooden darning egg at it and killed it dead as a doornail."

"It wasn't a wooden egg, Calista, it was ivory."

"No, no, I mean the wooden one before she got the ivory one, remember? It was dark wood. Anyhow it was a crazy dream, because she was real old, and you and I and Howie were just little kids." She turned to Agatha. "It was crazy seeing her old like that and we were just kids, but it wasn't as crazy as the time I dreamed she was dead in her coffin and she looked about twenty. Now *that* was a crazy dream." Calista went on in this vein until Agatha expected Dort to stop her with some remark of surprising candor.

Which she did: "We don't wash clothes around here till we run out of underwear!"

Taking her sister's interruption as the rebuke it was, Calista subsided, her story trailing off and ending in a sigh.

"You've *got* to stop talking about *death* all the time."

Calista nodded submissively as the door opened and in came their brother, a small, wiry man with thick glasses, a pouty lower lip, and the habit of speaking with great breathy force. Before Agatha or Frederick could greet him, he said, "I hated school all the way through from first grade till I was sixteen and dropped out. I could write, I could spell, I could read," he assured Agatha, pulling a chair up beside Frederick, "and that's all I needed, so why did I have to take all those years of school?"

Agatha understood that Howard Holister was part of that fraction of the population for whom the sight of one of his former teachers incited painful memories. She scowled at him, to show she wasn't daunted.

"And another thing—big words. Who puts out those big words anyway? If you can't talk without usin' words like that, then you ain't got nothin' to say."

"I myself didn't care much for the study of language until I got to college," Agatha confided. "You see we had the most boring language teacher in high school."

"But what about big words?" asked Howie, pleased to be taken seriously. "You had to know big words to be a teacher."

"A certain number, yes. But, Howard, there's nothing intrinsically wrong with big—"

"'Intrinsically'—oh, no!" He looked anguished. "You know what it seems like to me, Miss McGee? Seems to me they put out big words just to see if they'll catch on. 'Intrinsically' and such. I mean they aren't written down anywhere, they're just put out like fish bait. They got a new word out now; I heard it on the radio the other day." He paused for effect, then uttered it: "taxpert."

"Oh? I haven't heard that one," said Agatha.

"No, it's just out."

"Meaning tax expert, I suppose."

"Sure, anybody can figure out what it means."

"But it's not a *big* word."

"But it's a fancy word, and what do we need it for? You won't catch me sayin' it. Let's see, I heard another one, too, even worse." He gulped his drink, trying to call the other word to mind. He failed. He asked Frederick, "You folks come out here to get away from the flood?"

"Nope."

Dort said, "They came out to pay us a call, Howie, aren't they nice?"

"Well, I was gonna say, if they plan on stayin' overnight, it's gonna be pretty close quarters. We only got the two bedrooms." He turned again to Frederick. "Must seem funny, don't it, not being out on your route today?"

"Yep."

"Just my luck it floods on my day off. Just my luck it'll probably be nice and normal Monday and I'll have to go out as usual. Havin' a rural route is the most boring job in the world. Miss McGee, did I ever tell you what a boring life I lead?"

"Yes, many times."

"Funny how it works. You quit high school and you don't know where you're headed so you go in the army. You get out of the army and you still don't know where you're headed so you take the first job that comes along, in Dillon's Feed Mill. You get laid off that job and you take another one, out at the potato plant, and you don't like it so you quit, and you take other jobs like that and you still don't know where you're headed, until finally you go in with your sister when she becomes postmistress. So now it's twenty-three years here, and I finally know where I'm headed—I'm deliverin' mail for the rest of my workin' days."

"So?" said Agatha impatiently. "What's your point?"

He raised his voice. "So my point is, when you're young you wish you knew where you were headed, and then when you're older you wish you didn't."

"Oh, it's quite the opposite with me," she told him. "I knew where I was going from the time I was in Sister Hedwig's fifth grade. You girls remember what a crackerjack of a teacher she was." Dort and Calista nodded, smiling at the pleasant memory. "I was ten and decided I would come back to St. Isidore's and teach, and I did. It was only later in life I didn't know where I was headed. I'll never forget the loss I felt when St. Isidore's closed down. I was principal at the time. My forty-ninth year working in the same building. And it was up to me to call the plumber and have him drain the pipes. And the power company and have them turn off the electricity. And I had to disconnect the telephones and pull the shades. The worst part was pulling the shades, for some reason. It was the most beautiful sunny spring day. I just hated going around to every room . . . closing the windows and pulling the shades."

"Oops," said Frederick, rising from his chair. "Guess we better go." He pointed outdoors to a spot where water was beginning to flow across the alley.

Once again Agatha urged all three of them to come and stay at her house, and again they refused.

"That's nothin' to get excited about," said Howie. "The water's done risin'."

"We better go." Frederick gave Agatha a look so urgent it pulled her upright.

She gulped down the last of her tea and headed for the door. "Sorry to rush off, girls. Come to town and see me now."

"But we haven't had our pie yet," said Calista.

"Oh, stay at least for pie and coffee," urged Dort. "Calista made apple pie especially for you."

"Sorry, but Frederick knows best." She hurried down the steps to the car. "Good-bye Calista, good-bye Dort, good-bye Howard. Let's pray we aren't all inundated."

"That's the word!" said Howie. "'Inundated!' Heard it on the news this morning. If it means flooded, why can't they say flooded? Ticks me off the way—"

She and Frederick shut their doors and drove away.

Agatha, riding home over the wet roads, recalled her formative years, when she often heard her father speak with respect of William B. Holister, a Willoughby farmer and hardworking functionary of the Democratic party. He sent his children to Staggerford for their elementary education because Willoughby had no parochial school. His political diligence paid off a generation later when the postmaster general put his daughter Dort in charge of the Willoughby post office. This proved fortuitous all around. Dort, with the help of her sister, became a most efficient mail handler, keeping their cantankerous brother out of mischief, and keeping Willoughby on the map years after its expected demise—to say nothing of rescuing the three Holisters from misery and maybe even bankruptcy, since none of them knew the first thing about farming.

"Poor Calista," said Agatha.

Frederick made a sound of agreement, shook his head, and added, "Arthritis."

But it was not arthritis she was thinking about. She was remembering a time years ago when there was talk of Calista Holister, then nearing forty, marrying Andrew Jordan. Had that come to pass, there'd have been no need for the postmaster general to intercede for the Holisters, because Andrew Jordan was simply the most prosperous farmer in the southern half of Berrington County. Agatha had heard it said that Andrew could grow alfalfa out of stone. He'd bought many small farms, torn down the buildings, burned off the windbreaks, and put every square yard under cultivation. Why, there were cornfields around here—to look at them you'd swear you were someplace in Iowa.

But of course poor Calista would have come to grief with Andrew Jordan. Even as a sixth grader in Agatha's room, besides being thoughtless of others, Andrew had been a volatile and unrepentant truant. Lucky for Calista he didn't wait until it was too late, but showed his true colors before they were to be married. It was twenty-five years ago that that loose woman Susie Botz came between them and broke up their engagement. That was the year Susie Botz gave birth to her daughter Amy out of wedlock, and the night Amy was born, Andrew Jordan and a dentist from Loomis had a fistfight on the steps of Mercy Hospital, both claiming to be the father.

News like that traveled fast. By the next morning—it was Sunday—everybody in town knew about the fistfight and the Holisters heard about it coming out of late mass in Willoughby. Calista of course was devastated. Dort phoned Agatha who drove out to their farm and tried to comfort her. She also tried, and failed, not to tell her "I told you so," which was the wrong thing to say, because Calista increased her moaning and weeping and carrying on until Agatha had to leave the house. She knew it was twenty-five years ago because she saw a birthday ad last month in the *Staggerford Weekly* that said,

Amy Jordan
Sakes alive
you're twenty-five.

———

*All your friends at
the potato plant.*

Amy had been given the Jordan name, which was curious because she was said to resemble the dentist more than she did Andrew Jordan, and neither man ever married Susie Botz.

"I've been told that Amy has finally found a settled life for her-self," Agatha blurted aloud in the car, confusing Frederick.

"Amy?" he asked, eyeing a water-covered dip in the road ahead.

"Amy Jordan. With her third husband. He's a foreman at the potato plant. But no one seems to know what became of Susie."

"Susie?"

"Susie Botz. Her mother." She was about to reprimand Fred-erick for letting his brain grow lazy when she realized he'd been gone—to Vietnam—during the Susie Botz era. "Do you ever hear the name Susie Botz brought up at the pool hall?"

"Nope," he lied. At the pool hall, though she hadn't been seen for years, Susie Botz's name had come to symbolize the fallen woman, but French, driving slowly through the water and out the other side, knew better than to speak of such things to Agatha.

River Street was blocked off, but the policeman standing guard, at Agatha's insistence, let Frederick's Oldsmobile through the barri-cade. Sara Meers, her goddaughter, stepped out into the street, stop-ping the car, to tell Agatha that the state engineer—Harry, the same man her brother spoke of at lunch—had revised his estimate upward because of the steady rain. "We're sandbagging River Street, and we got loads more sandbags coming in," she proclaimed with glee, "and even then we're not sure it's enough. You and us and everybody along River Street might have to leave home for a night or two."

But Sara's warning went unheeded by Agatha, because, glanc-ing up at her front porch, she saw a figure standing at her door, a woman shaking out an umbrella and wearing a coat that reached down to her shoe tops. She couldn't make out her face at this distance.

"Who is it, Frederick?"

"A stranger."

He pulled up to the curb and she ordered him to honk as Sara was called back to her sandbags.

The woman had a style about her uncommon in Staggerford. Her long raincoat and umbrella were a matching shade of taupe, and Agatha caught a glimpse of patterned stockings as she came down the steps toward the car. Leaning in at the driver's window, she revealed a necklace of gold. "Do you know who lives here?" she asked. She had a large, wide-eyed face with deep dimples. She was perhaps fifty-five years old.

"I live here," said Agatha. "My name is McGee."

"Well, I just moved in down the street, and I thought I should ask my neighbors before I let them go ahead and flood my basement. I've bought the Ferguson house. My name is Linda Schwartzman."

Frederick briefly took the hand she offered and handed it along to Agatha.

"Oh, yes, your husband is our new undertaker," said Agatha, recalling a recent ad in the *Weekly* concerning a name change at the local mortuary. Formerly the Carlson-Case Funeral Home, it was to be known henceforth as the Case-Schwartzman Funeral and Cremation Service.

"No," said the woman. "I am unmarried."

"Well, your brother or father then," Agatha insisted, eager to show that she stayed abreast of the news.

The woman emitted a jolly laugh. "No, no, *I* am the mortician."

"You!" Agatha was ready to laugh along with her until she realized the woman wasn't joking. "You?"

"Mr. Carlson is retiring, and so Mr. Case and I will be partners when he gets back from his European vacation. I'm happy to meet you Mrs. McGee, Mr. McGee."

"No, no. I, too, am unmarried, Miss Schwartzman. This is my nephew Frederick Lopat."

Again the full-throated laugh. Then, "Are you going to let them flood your basement, Miss McGee?"

"Flood my basement? I don't understand."

She explained that the city clerk, a man named Mulholland, had been visiting houses along the river and recommending that those with old, unfortified foundations have their basements filled with water to withstand the pressure the flood was certain to exert. "He says our foundations will collapse inward if we don't."

"Nonsense," said Agatha. "Please come into my house. I'll get the city clerk on the phone."

Frederick helped Agatha indoors and hung up the coats of the two women; then, while he drove around to the alley and into the garage, Agatha, going to her window chair, phoned city hall and asked for William Mulholland. "He has a one-track mind," she confided to Linda Schwartzman. "He was the same as a sixth grader. Gets an idea in his head and never lets it go. Do sit down."

Her guest took the chair she pointed to—Father Healy's chair nearby—and looked around at the many admirable pieces of very old furniture. A book collector, Linda Schwartzman was especially taken by the matching set of free-standing, glassed-in bookcases.

"William. Agatha McGee. What's all this foolishness about flooding people's basements?"

The Ferguson house, though larger, didn't have the potential of the McGee house, Ms. Schartzman decided, didn't have the grace, the feeling of spaciousness. It lacked the wide windows giving out on a large yard.

"William, with all due respect to your colleagues on the Mississippi flood plain . . . I have to say it's an idea I've never heard of before. And what happens to everything we have stored in our cellars? Do you think . . . ?"

But these rooms, despite the windows, had a rather gloomy aspect on days like this. Ms. Schwartzman would start by painting the dark oak woodwork white and laying down a cream-colored carpet.

After a few more words with the city clerk, including, "But I sit high above my neighbors and I have a *strong* foundation!" Agatha hung up and turned to her guest. "The bigwigs at city hall are expecting trouble. William Mulholland claims what I don't for a minute believe. He says there's a chance all of us along River Street . . . will wake up the day after tomorrow with water up to our windowsills. Those with weak foundation walls can save them by equalizing the pressure from within. He says it won't be necessary in my case, because my foundation is made of stone. My guess is that yours is, too, Miss Schwartzman, so let's have a cup of tea . . . and watch the water come up." Agatha headed for the kitchen.

"But mine isn't stone. It's a thin wall of cement."

"The Ferguson house? But it must be stone. It went up at the same time this one did."

"No, the engineer examined my basement."

Agatha stopped and considered this. "I see. Well, the Fergusons were very thrifty people. They employed my father as their attorney and he always had trouble collecting his fees."

While Agatha prepared tea, her guest roamed the living room, looking at the pictures and plaques on the walls. One in particular captured her attention, a group photo of elderly people standing under a canopy displaying the words "Shea Hall."

"Is that picture taken at Rookery State College?" she asked later, squeezing lemon into her teacup.

Agatha squinted across the room. "Yes, that was taken about ten years ago. They gathered a bunch of us has-beens together for the dedication of their new education building."

"I wondered. And is it named after Professor Simon Shea by any chance?"

Agatha nodded. "The Simon P. Shea Teaching and Learning Center."

Linda Schwartzman returned to the photo for another look. "That's Simon, the tall gentleman standing at the back, right?"

"Yes, he was as famous as teachers get, in his day. You knew him, did you?"

"Oh, yes, he taught me . . . so much."

Agatha, busily fussing over her tea, didn't notice Linda Schwartzman's agitation, wasn't aware of how close she was standing to the photo, memorizing every detail of the old man's face. Agatha was not aware, of course, that this new neighbor of hers, when her name was Linda Mayo, had once been, very briefly, during a trip to Ireland, the professor's lover.

Agatha did notice, however, how suddenly thoughtful and distracted the woman seemed, returning to her chair and looking out at the rain. Miss Schwartzman was remembering her regret at waiting until she was a senior before enrolling in one of Simon's classes. Had she known him earlier she would have taken every subject he taught merely to be in the same room with such a gentleman.

"And where do you come from, Miss Schwartzman, if you don't mind my asking?"

"Fostoria, Ohio, though I grew up here in Minnesota." She managed to pull her attention back to her tea and her elderly hostess. "After college I was a flight attendant for a time, then went back to school in mortuary science."

"It strikes me as an odd field for a woman."

"Well, you see, I'd married Manny Schwartzman. He was an undertaker whose father owned three funeral homes in Ohio."

"And he prevailed upon you . . ."

"Oh, Manny was a prevailer all right—that's why I divorced him—but he didn't dictate my choice of vocation. No, when I saw the Schwartzman operation, it was entirely my idea to take up mortuary science. It's work I'm suited for."

"How so? It strikes me as so . . ." She meant, but didn't want to say, ghoulish.

"What I mean is, helping people through their grief. I discovered I have a talent for consoling people."

Agatha could see it. The woman, like Father Healy, had compassionate eyes. But they contained something painful as well, like regret or sadness, perhaps the residue from her divorce.

"And do you have children?"

"No, we had no children. We were only married for a little over a year."

"Oh, then you've been single a long time."

The woman only nodded.

Probably twenty years, Agatha calculated. Flight attendants used to lose their jobs in their thirties, when they lost their figures. Agatha drew herself up in her chair, tightened her lips, and said, "Well, I've never regretted the single life."

How untrue this was. Linda Schwartzman could sense, could see in the old woman's face a kind of forceful bullying of past events to conform to some ideal.

How untrue it was, Agatha realized after her guest had left. There were fleeting regrets in her thirties and forties, every time she met Preston Warner on the street—the man whose proposal she'd turned down in her twenties. And regret returned in her late sixties when she began meeting and kept bidding good-bye to James O'Hannon, the Irish priest who won her heart. Oh, this latter regret was very intense and lasted well beyond James's death four years ago; it actually lasted, at a reduced level, to this very day. So what possessed her to blurt out that falsehood to Miss Schwartzman? It was the first lie of her life.

She called to Janet in her room upstairs and invited her into the kitchen for a cup of tea. Frederick came in from the garage and reported that he had been talking to Imogene Kite across the alley. Imogene, having changed her mind since this morning, had decided to worry about the flood. She'd come home early to make sure the sandbaggers were doing their job.

"Tut, tut," said Agatha, refusing to worry, "Imogene's always been something of an alarmist. You aren't worried, are you, Frederick?"

"No," he said, but the uncertainty in his eyes prompted her to review the two principal reasons not to fret:

"High water has never been a threat in the past, Frederick. And even if the Badbattle overflows, you are living in the highest house in the neighborhood."

"Yeah," he said, looking slightly less fretful. "We don't have a floor drain down the basement, do we?"

"No floor drain. Yet how I wished we had one in the days of the wringer washing machine. Every wash day I had to corral some man to carry my tubs of water up the steps and pour them outside. Imogene's father Lyle did it until he died. And then my lodger Miles Pruitt did it until *he* died. My, how he hated that job." She chuckled at the memory. "And after that there was a series of other lodgers, until I put in my automatic washer and dryer."

Janet said, "Why do you ask, Fredriko?"

"'Cuz Imogene says every house in the neighborhood is supposed to have its lowest drains plugged, to keep sewage from backing up into their basements."

"What a horrible prospect," said Agatha. "You'll have a cup of tea, Frederick?"

"No, I gotta go to the lumber yard and get a seven-foot two-by-four."

"Whatever for?"

"'Cause Imogene asked me to plug her drain for her, and her basement ceiling's seven feet tall." Though addressing Agatha, he spoke to Janet because she was easier to talk to; she had a noncritical way of looking at people. Maybe it was simply old age, but Agatha had a skeptical set to her face all the time. "See, that's how you keep the drain plug in place; you brace it against the ceiling with a two-by-four. That way the sewer water can't force its way in."

After Frederick left for the lumber yard and Janet for the grocery store, a strange excitement swept over Agatha, a feeling of euphoric well-being, which, when she analyzed it, stemmed from her role as hostess. She couldn't remember when she last had had company, but the prospect of overnight guests stirred up a kind of joy that made her wonder if she was wrong to spend most of her life alone. The family she grew up in had been so dear to her, why had she not then provided herself with a family of her own? As a girl she'd been attached so strongly to her mother that she developed an inordinate fear of separation. She remembered how hard it was to leave home at six and start school, and she remembered the tragedy that struck her in the first grade.

It was perhaps two weeks into the school year and, by swallowing her fear, she'd only just begun to feel at home in Sister Simona's classroom, when she looked out the window and saw her mother walking along the sunny street without her daughter. Horrors, she was going downtown and leaving Agatha behind in this chalk-smelling room and with all these kids whose mothers probably had never taken them downtown in their lives. She left her desk and ran to the window and Sister Simona intercepted her. Her cry of grief must have been bloodcurdling, because the old nun dragged her out into the hallway where she stood shuddering and weeping into the heavy folds of Sister's habit. The nun's hands on Agatha's shoulders were comforting. When she finally gained control of herself Sister gave her one of her rare smiles and led her back to her place in the classroom. "What in the heck was that all about?" whispered Leonard Stillings who sat behind her. Agatha didn't answer. Leonard was too heartless, too much the mischief-maker to understand mother love. Besides, he was beneath her, because Sister's smile had raised her to a plane far above most of her classmates. She was now one of Sister's favorites.

But Sister Simona had no favorites, a fact Agatha was shocked to discover the next Monday morning when, after their opening prayer and Pledge of Allegiance, she declared, for everyone in the room to hear, "Agatha McGee, I don't want to see you being naughty at Sunday mass again." Naughty? What could she mean? Never in her six years of life had Agatha knowingly been naughty at mass—or anywhere else for that matter. All day she devoted her powers of concentration to reviewing her behavior in church, but to no avail. It wasn't until the following Sunday morning, back at mass with the rest of the first grade under Sister's watchful eye, that she recalled accidentally dropping her Sunday offering envelope onto the floor and causing the usher with the collection basket to wait five seconds while she picked it up. Here then was a form of naughtiness she hadn't been aware of—precipitating a hitch in holy liturgy.

Later, when she was an elementary teacher herself, it was Sister Simona's refusal to play favorites that Agatha most admired in retrospect and tried to imitate. Looking back, she decided that she was successfully evenhanded throughout her long career, except in certain cases where students needed special encouragement—students like Janet and her sisters because she knew what a hopeless, motherless household they came from, and Frederick because he was her nephew.

. . .

After dinner, phone calls kept Agatha and Janet busy into the evening. Janet called her father to warn him, in case her sister LeeAnn hadn't, not to come into town until the water went down. His farm was well out of harm's way, up in the hardscrabble hills west of town, but he didn't always keep up with current events. Then she called her house on the river to see if Stephen was home yet. He answered, reassuring her that all was well at the house, but the only road to it would certainly be under water before long. Wouldn't he like to come and stay at Agatha's rather than be cut off from civilization? No, he had a test to study for and there were lots of pizzas in the freezer. Next she dialed her husband Randy's number in Rookery to tell him that the road home might be submerged, so he might as well stay put. She didn't reach him at his Rookery lodging, The Red Roof Motel, so she left her message with the desk clerk.

Agatha was on the receiving end. William Mulholland called to say that if electrical and telephone service in her neighborhood were to be cut off without warning, it would happen on Sunday when the flood reached Staggerford. She had one day to make provisions or else leave her house. He urged her to do the latter. Agatha thanked him for the message and told him once again that her house was higher than all the other properties on River Street, and she hung up. Lillian called to say she couldn't come over tomorrow; Imogene wanted to take her out to lunch and then shopping for shoes. Father Healy called to check on her health—he'd only then seen the newspaper. She dismissed this topic with a "Tut, Father," and went on to say she hoped his Communion visit wouldn't be put off in the morning by his fear of high water, because she had something very important to talk to him about.

SATURDAY

"No, not a lie," insisted Father Healy the next morning. "Not even a fib."

"Oh, indeed it was, Father. It was a false statement and I need forgiveness before I can take Communion. You see, I believe I have regretted the single life since I was sixty-eight. And yet I denied it to my neighbor."

"No, no, you're much too hard on yourself, Miss McGee. You said it came out unexpectedly. You didn't mean to say it."

"But I said it."

"So what? In order to commit a sin you need volition of the will. You know that, certainly." The priest decided that, more than forgiveness, this woman needed to relieve herself of a story, and so he risked prying. "What happened when you were sixty-eight, Miss McGee?"

Her first response was a fierce scowl, but then, as though she could not contain it any longer, the story came pouring out. Upon her retirement from the classroom she made a trip to Ireland to meet a man who had won her heart through several years of written correspondence. During a day or two spent in Dublin together, they proved to be extremely compatible, and Agatha realized, really for the first time, how deeply happy she might have been with a partner through life. She began to imagine herself married to him. It didn't occur to her at the time to wonder why such a marriageable man had never married. The reason, as she was soon to discover, was that he was a priest.

At this point in her telling, she paused to look outside, and her head began its tremor. Father Healy, too, looked out at the weather—a dry day, with high, broken clouds—and patiently waited.

Some years passed with scarcely a word written between them, she said, and then on a trip she took to Italy, this very man—his name was James O'Hannon—turned up at her hotel. She discovered that her feeling for him was undiminished; indeed, it was deepened because he'd been diagnosed with cancer. She invited him to tag along with her tour group, which he did, and they proved to be kindred spirits.

"And you loved him?" Father Healy prompted.

"I said we were kindred spirits." She kept her eyes averted. "But he died."

Another very long pause.

"His brother Matt phoned me one morning and told me. Said he'd have phoned earlier but he didn't want to wake me. Well, Matt isn't the brightest bulb in Ireland. If he'd called me the moment James died, at 3:00 A.M. his time, I'd have been eating my supper. As it was, the call came at two in the morning my time, but never mind. The funeral was set for Friday, three days hence, and I said I was coming over for it.

"It was Epiphany week, the very worst time to book a flight to Ireland. Hundreds of college students from the Midwest were on the loose for the month of January and flocking to Europe. Our local librarian Imogene Kite, who doubles as our local travel agent—a real numbskull—suggested I go standby. But another agent . . . a bright young thing from Garvey Travel in Rookery, advised against it. There were already people waiting to fill every empty seat, this young woman said. And furthermore she didn't think I'd like hanging around the Rookery airport for hours. The best she could do was a flight to Ireland, by way of Chicago and Cincinnati, leaving Thursday afternoon."

"I'll bet I know who that young woman was in Rookery," said Father Healy. "Her name was Verna Jessen, wasn't it?"

"Why would I remember a thing like that? Anyhow I phoned Matt and asked him to do everything in his power to put the funeral off until Saturday, since I wasn't going to arrive at the Dublin airport until ten o'clock in the morning on Friday, and Dublin was sixty miles from Kilrath. He told me not to worry, the funeral was to be held in the Procathedral in Dublin. 'Matt, you don't understand,' I said to him, 'it takes hours to get out of a plane and retrieve your luggage and find a taxi. And what's the funeral doing in Dublin? His grave's in Kilrath.' Matt explained that his brother in death had become suddenly famous enough to be recognized by the Bishop of Dublin, who had taken up James's cause.

"You see, James O'Hannon, in retirement, began to evangelize against the violence erupting in Northern Ireland. And he did this for four years, at no little risk of his life. Traveling the length and breadth of Ireland, until his death from cancer."

Agatha said she'd flown to Ireland five times and accompanied him on his speaking tours, at first as his driver and finally as his driver, dresser, and nurse, because he refused to give up the cause until he could scarcely get out of bed anymore. "He died an unknown hero, I thought, in the room he'd been born in . . . above O'Hannon's Pub in the village of Kilrath."

The plane was late leaving Chicago, but she was able to catch her flight out of Cincinnati, and, lo and behold, she was upgraded to first class. Still, she fretted all the way across the Atlantic, certain she was making the trip for nothing. "But there were signs of success. The first sign came when the flight attendant served a drink James was very fond of. I forget the name of it, champagne and orange juice."

"Mimosa."

"Yes, that's it. Well, I didn't think so much about it at the time, but I've asked others and everyone is surpised. In the history of aviation, nobody, it seems, has ever been served that drink on an airplane." She studied her guest. "Have you?"

"No, never."

"The second sign was when our flight attendant in first class— whose father's name was James O'Bannon, incidentally, a strikingly similar name—said she lived near the Procathedral. She knew of a street that had just opened up after months of repairs and it was a shorter way from the airport. She drew me a map to give the taxi driver in case he didn't know about it. She saw to it that I was the first one off the plane and told me where to find a taxi. To make a long story slightly less long, I got to the church before James did. I wondered, when I first went in, whether Matt had given me a bum steer. But more and more people gathered and then his coffin was brought in and placed feet first toward the altar. And then it was opened up. And at eleven-twenty mass began.

"It was a glorious mass. None of your shortcuts, a solemn high mass with a great crowd of men and boys on the altar and clouds of incense and a tenor singing 'Panis Angelicus' beautiful enough to break your . . ."

After a long silence, Father Healy asked, "And how long ago was this?"

"Four years, come summer."

She turned to catch the surprise in his eyes. "Yes, I know, I was much more vigorous then. These last years have been hard on me. 'Do it before you turn seventy-five,' I told Lillian the other day. 'Otherwise it won't get done.' And then I realized Lillian is my age exactly. I envy her her stamina. And that's another sin I want to confess, my jealousy of everyone younger than I am."

"It's natural to regret growing old."

Since there was no changing the man's mind, she changed her tactic. "Well then, I would like you to give me general absolution for any sins of my past life that I may have forgotten to confess." Surely this would wipe away yesterday's falsehood and her ongoing envy.

But Father Healy refused to do even this, claiming that he didn't want to encourage her in the fussy direction she seemed to be going. "You're much too smart a woman to become so narrow, Miss McGee. I've known certain people who declined into scrupulosity as they grew older, and they spent their last years on earth examining their consciences instead of living."

"I've known them, too, Father. They're called saints."

After communion, which she reluctantly and solemnly took at Father Healy's insistence, she was on her way to the kitchen to brew him a cup of tea when she heard someone pounding heavily on the back door. She called up the stairway to Frederick, hoping he would answer it, but Janet came down instead, brushing past Agatha, giving her a peck on the cheek, and went out through the kitchen to the back porch. There was a mumbled conversation out there that Agatha couldn't make out, and then Janet reappeared with a stranger in tow, a black-haired woman obviously of Indian ancestry smiling a self-conscious smile and advancing toward Agatha with her arms out. Seeing Agatha stiffen, she stopped and lost her smile, and that's when Agatha recognized her. "Beverly, Beverly," she said, stepping forward and taking the woman in her arms. "I didn't know you, and do you know why? Because as a girl you never smiled."

Janet had heard enough about Beverly Bingham to know she had little to smile about as a girl—one of two sisters reared in the gulch west of town by a murderous mother. How awful, she thought, taking the woman's hand as Agatha introduced her. Father Healy, hearing the voices, put his head in at the kitchen door and tried to excuse himself, claiming he had other shut-ins to visit, but Agatha wouldn't hear of it.

"Father, you have to come and meet my surrogate daughter from years ago. Sit down here and get acquainted with her, Father. She has much to teach us about the world at large . . . because she traveled most of it when her husband was a soldier. You used to see kangaroos along the highways, didn't you, Beverly? I have kept the postcards you sent me.

"And this is Janet Meers, Father," she continued, placing her guests around the kitchen table. "Surely you know Louise and Carl Meers of Meers Realty."

The priest looked bewildered.

"They met you at the Knights of Columbus banquet," Janet prompted.

"Ah, yes," he said, not remembering, "and you are their daughter, I take it."

"No, no," said Agatha. "Janet is their daughter-in-*law,* married to their son, Randy."

Once she had the tea and gingersnaps set before them, Agatha was able finally to concentrate on Beverly, to study her troubled, uncared-for face. This was the girl who came to live with her after her mother had been sent to the State Hospital for the Criminally Insane for shooting Miles Pruitt, Agatha's lodger. This was the girl who, before the murder, used to drop in for visits and her remarks were so crude and candid that Agatha was taken aback. She recalled one sunny autumn day in particular when Beverly, smoking a cigarette, advised her concerning the women's movement. "In your day women were down more," she declared, and Agatha asked, "And now we're up?" The girl replied, "Well, at least now we're on our way," and she held out her cigarette as proof. Agatha smiled now at the memory, but her smile was soon replaced by a frown as she remembered the heart-wrenching grief they shared at Miles Pruitt's funeral and afterward, through the winter and spring, until Beverly graduated and was whisked away by her soldier boy. She recalled how crying used to alter the lines of Beverly's face, giving her the aspect of the older woman she'd since become.

As Janet and Father Healy carried on a stilted conversation about real estate values, Agatha sensed a nervous urgency underneath the demure smile Beverly kept giving her. She realized that the girl had come back into her life for some sort of solace, not a tea party. Why had she asked the priest to join them? Didn't she know he'd make conversation stiff and difficult?

"I'm sorry to be keeping you from your rounds of shut-ins," she told him. "But I wanted you at least to meet two of my favorite people in the world."

Recognizing this as a sign of dismissal, the priest swiftly vanished, allowing Beverly to open up. She had no trouble telling her story in front of Janet, whom she had only met ten minutes before, because Janet had such a friendly, unthreatening look. She said that for the past year or more, ever since marrying a man named Cooper and then divorcing him, she'd been living in Berrington, barely forty miles north of Staggerford. "Why, in heaven's name, has it taken a year for you to come and see me?" Agatha wanted to know. "All this while I was imagining you in Timbuktu."

"I meant to come as soon as I got my life in order, but . . ." A helpless shrug. Once again the small, uneasy smile.

"Do you mean it's not in order yet?"

"God, no, it's a mess. You see, I've got Owen on my hands again. He's psychotic half the time."

"And Owen is . . . ?"

"My son. Owen. He's twenty-one. He's been living in a halfway house in Berrington and doing better lately. No episodes since Christmastime. And so, this week, I thought as long as he was due for an outing, the two of us would come and visit you. This was the day before yesterday. It was late when we left Berrington, so B.W. released Owen for overnight so we could stay at the Thrifty Springs and come and see you yesterday morning. I met B.W. last year, when Owen first went in the halfway house."

"And B.W. is . . . ?"

"He manages the halfway house. B.W. Cooper. He was my husband for eight months, my second husband." She didn't pause for comments or questioning, but pressed on. "But Owen started having an episode in the motel, and so instead of coming here I had to hightail it back to his halfway house in Berrington. Then this morning I came back to Staggerford to see you, Miss McGee. But the flood is moving downstream, and I'll never get out of town till the water goes down. I stopped at Thrifty Springs to try to book a room, but it's full of people running away from the flood."

"You will stay here, Beverly."

"Oh thank you, Miss McGee, I was hoping. Just like old times."

"Not quite. Janet and her daughter are in your old room. You'll have the small bedroom at the end of the hall upstairs."

"Oh thank you, thank you," she repeated, leaning into Agatha, and Agatha, never much of a hugger, leaned into her, hugging her tightly.

Then, in through the back door, to Agatha's surprise, stepped her nephew.

"Frederick, I thought you were in bed." He'd never been an early riser.

"I been up the street, helpin' 'em sandbag."

"Frederick, this is my old friend, Beverly Bingham. She says the roads are under water."

"In places, they say." He couldn't help staring at this daughter of the murdering mother he'd heard so much about.

Beverly, ignoring his gaze, was about to continue her story when the phone in the other room rang, and Frederick went to answer it. He called to Agatha. She was gone only a minute before the two of them returned with worry and urgency written on their faces.

"Tell them, Frederick. I'm sorry, girls, we have to leave for a while." She hurried off to fetch her raincoat.

"An old friend of Agatha's in Willoughby," he told them. "She died."

The highway was closed where Frederick earlier drove through water, but fortunately he was familiar with the secondary roads in this area, and they arrived in Willoughby before the doctor, the priest, or the undertaker. The lowest streets were flooded, but Main Street was still high above danger. They found Calista in hysterics, as Agatha had expected, and her brother pacing about their living quarters, claiming that Dort's death marked the end of their livelihood—he and his surviving sister would have to vacate the post office and move to the poor farm.

"Nonsense," Agatha told him. "The poor farm doesn't exist any more. Frederick, take him out front, would you? He's disturbing Calista. No, on second thought, take him for a ride in the car. We can't have him upsetting the whole town."

"But it's Saturday morning," said Frederick. "The place is open for business."

"Close it." She steered Frederick to the front and then asked, "Where is she?"

Howie pointed to his sisters' bedroom, and there she found Dort Holister in her nightgown and robe and lying on top of her quilt with a bloody leg and her good eye half open. Agatha had seen any number of dead bodies in her lifetime, beginning with her brother, dead of influenza when she was eight, but nobody ever looked as inert, as lifeless, as Dort. She lay with one arm awkwardly bent back under her. She was cold to the touch. Agatha closed her eyelid and picked her glasses with the frosted lens off the bedside table. "What happened?" she asked.

Calista and Howie, remaining well away from the bedroom, both answered at once, but their story was the same. Dort went out on the stoop, they said, to bring in the morning mailbag—the truck left it off on its way through town at around 4:00 A.M.—and she collapsed in the doorway. Calista found her when she got up to see where the chilly draft was coming from. She said the step was icy and Dort had evidently slipped and hit her head. Howie said no, she had a stroke.

"But there was blood," cried Calista.

"The blood was on her shinbone, don't be stupid!"

Calista appealed to Agatha with her eyes. *You see how he is. What am I going to do?*

"How did she get from the stoop into the bedroom?" Agatha wanted to know.

"I carried her," said Howie proudly.

"And why was there blood?"

"Why? Why! What are you, the police? The coroner? How do I know why there was blood? Jesus Martha, maybe she cut her leg on the edge of the step when she fell down. The step is cement."

Through the door they heard voices in the post office. "That will be Billy and Inga from across the street," said Calista. "I called them."

The door opened and Frederick ushered in Billy and Inga Wentworth, proprietors of Jiffystop, Willoughby's only gas station and food market. They were a mismatched couple, both in size and temperament. Billy was short, round, and shy. Irma was tall and bubbly. "Why, Agatha McGee," she exclaimed, embracing her, "I heard you were out here yesterday. How wonderful to see you up and around." Then she took Calista in her arms. Smiling through her tears, she crooned, "There, there, my dear. There, there. There, there."

Billy sidled up to Howie, and Agatha heard him say, "Thought she was dyin'."

"She's dead as can be," Howie told him.

"No, I mean her," Billy nodded in Agatha's direction.

"Her? Naw. She ain't dyin'."

"The paper said."

"What paper?"

"The *Weekly*."

"Aw, who reads that rag? It's only words."

Next, in through the back door came Benji Simms, who operated Benji's Beer Bar next door, and Samantha Edgerton of Samantha's Donut Shop down the block. Samantha bore a plate heaped with sugared donuts. Benji Simms was an edgy man— though not so antagonistic as Howie Holister—with a carelessly clipped beard and a left ear that stuck out much farther than his right. He was a bachelor whose rumpled clothes had never struck Agatha as perfectly clean. "How are you, Miss McGee?" he asked. "I hear you haven't been feelin' the best."

"Perfectly fine," she told him, turning away from his odor of stale beer and cigarette smoke.

Samantha Edgerton, a tall, fading beauty whose awkwardness had always made Agatha uneasy for some odd reason, shook

Agatha's hand while setting her plate of pastries on the dining table. She was a newcomer to the area, having moved there less than a dozen years ago from someplace up north. She said, meaning to be hopeful, "I had an uncle with congestive heart failure, Miss McGee, and he lived to be eighty-something."

Agatha's reply was designed to mortify the Donut Queen, as she was known in Willoughby. "So this will be the decade of my death, are you saying?" Agatha was nearly eighty.

The woman, having pegged Agatha at around age seventy, was momentarily flustered at having said something wrong. She stepped away to join the two other women. Calista was calmed by this roomful of friends. She set out mugs and a carafe of coffee. All partook, glad to have something to do with their hands, and retreated silently to their respective gender corners, men at the picture window, all of them staring out at the rare phenomenon of sunshine and shadow, women near the bedroom door, which stood slightly ajar, and allowed Inga Wentworth and the Donut Queen a glimpse of the body.

Agatha broke the silence. "We can't be lollygagging, my friends. They will be here any minute for the body. Before they get here we have to decide if Willoughby is worth saving."

"Willoughby's down the tubes," cried Howie Holister, despairing across the room.

"Shush!" ordered Agatha.

"Well, Dort's dead, ain't she? And the high muckety-mucks in Washington say the post office closes when she dies. So where does that leave us? Down the tubes, that's where."

"Howard, will you be quiet for a minute? There is a way."

He looked aggrieved. "I'm only saying the rest of us might as well be dead along with her."

Billy Wentworth, at the window, said, "Here comes the hearse."

Agatha turned her back on Howie, saying, "What I have in mind will require everyone in this room to keep a secret for as long as you live. So first of all, I want to know if you can do that."

"To save our town, sure," said Benji Simms.

Samantha Edgerton and Inga Wentworth nodded their agreement vigorously.

From her pocket, Agatha drew out Dort's glasses with the frosted lens. She held them up to Calista's face and said, "We tell them it's Calista who died, and Calista goes ahead playing Dort for the rest of her life."

The deputy coroner, Dr. Hammond, who diagnosed Agatha's dubious coronary weakness, arrived in the hearse with the undertaker's man. The doctor, a bearded, humorless young man not well acquainted with the Holisters, consulted with Dort's brother and sister until Calista withdrew in tears and assigned Agatha her spokesperson. Howie's theory—a fatal stroke—carried the day. All it took for Dr. Hammond to write *cerebral hemorrhage* on the death certificate was a nod of the head from Agatha when he inquired whether the deceased had suffered from high blood pressure, and an emphatic "Nosiree!" from Howie when asked if the family wished to have an autopsy performed. The undertaker's driver, unknown to Agatha and obviously new on the job, was much more interested in the mechanics of his gurney than the identity of the deceased. While the body was being wheeled out to the hearse, Father Healy phoned to say the highway was closed and he would administer the sacrament of the dying conditionally at the mortuary. Agatha was relieved when the hearse left town, because she knew that the priest had not yet been introduced to the Holisters, and that Bert Case was still on vacation, leaving his new partner Linda Schwartzman in charge of the body from then until it was buried. Her fabrication might save Willoughby after all. Calista was its only potential weakness.

"Calista, why don't you come home with me, at least until after the funeral."

Calista nodded eagerly and went to pack a suitcase.

Agatha next stilled Howie's objections by volunteering Frederick's help in running the post office for a week or so. "You can return after you take Calista and me into town, can't you, Frederick? You can move out here for a few days and keep Howard company."

Frederick nodded, not eagerly.

In the back seat of the Oldsmobile, Agatha comforted Calista as Frederick led the hearse back to town over bumpy gravel roads.

Gone scarcely more than an hour, Agatha arrived home to find Janet and Beverly still in the kitchen. They had been joined by Janet's daughter Sara, who like her mother appeared engrossed in a story Beverly was telling.

"But before that, he first flipped out a year or so earlier when he was sixteen," Beverly said of her son. "In school one day he got mad and blew up so bad that his shop teacher locked him in the paint-drying room. He should of taken him to the principal of course, but he claimed Owen was uncontrollable and the best he could do was back him into the paint-drying room and lock the door. Hi, Miss McGee, we were just comparing kids, Janet and I."

"What made him so mad?" Sara wanted to know.

"Probably one of his classmates. I forget. He used to have a terrible temper."

Agatha ushered Calista into the kitchen. "Girls, I want you to meet a friend of mine. Dort, this is Beverly Bingham and—"

"Beverly Cooper." Shaking the overwrought lady's weak, gloved hand, Beverly was intrigued by the frosted lens. "My dad had one eye," she said, "but he always wore a patch."

"And this is Janet Raft Meers."

"I live out your direction," said Janet. "I've seen you in the Willoughby Post Office."

"That was probably my sister." Calista, forgetting her role in the deception, managed to get this much out before dissolving in tears.

"And this is her daughter, Sara," said Agatha.

Sara, frightened by the old woman's weeping, shrank down in her chair.

"You girls will excuse us. Dort's sister has died and I've asked her to stay with me for a few days."

Janet jumped to her feet. "Do you have bags? Let me take them upstairs for you."

"No, Janet, I'm putting her in my bedroom down here. Frederick will bring in her bags."

"But where will you sleep?"

"I'll take Frederick's room. Frederick's going back to Willoughby . . . to stay with Howie at least through Monday . . . and help him run things."

"But she can have our room," Janet offered. "You've got a rollaway up there in the hallway that I can sleep on, and Sara can sleep down here on the couch."

"Mother! . . ." Her daughter's reaction was a look of such absolute anguish that the idea was immediately dropped, and the visitor, wiping her eyes, followed Agatha out of the kitchen.

"Misery, why is there so much misery in the world?" said Beverly. "Anyhow, when the class period ended, the shop teacher—Mr. Kling was his name—went to report Owen's behavior to the principal, and on his way he saw Owen going out the front door. Owen had broken out a window and run to his locker to get his coat and was on his way home."

Frederick came through, carrying Calista's baggage, and the two women and Sara left the kitchen table and moved into the living room. "So anyhow, I was called in by the principal to talk about Owen's fit of rage. The principal and Mr. Kling came on strong, said they intended to suspend Owen from school, and I came back at them just as strong. I said to the principal, sort of an elderly guy with a white mustache, I said, 'Listen here, your shop teacher here could've killed my boy by trapping him in that paint-drying room, and he only busted outa there to save his life, and if you suspend him I'm taking you to court.' Owen's real sensitive to fumes of any kind and paint fumes are just the worst. 'And another thing,' I said, 'how come there's a lock on that door in the first place?' And do you know what Mr. Kling told me? He said if they didn't keep their projects locked up while the paint's drying they'd get stolen by the end of the first day they're in there. 'Well, that's easy,' I said, 'catch whoever's doing the stealing and weed him out.' And Mr. Kling told me, I swear to God, he said this: 'It isn't just one person stealing, it's every boy and girl in this entire high school, stealing from one another.' Well, I just . . . I mean, doesn't that just shock you, Janet, to think the entire student body is a pack of thieves?"

"I don't know if I believe that." Janet looked at her daughter. "Is that true, honey, everybody in high school steals things?"

"They're all jerks," said Sara bitterly. "I wish I could get suspended."

Janet suggested to Sara, "How about going back outside? I'm sure they can use the help." Janet would have liked to tell Beverly more about her daughter, who was proving much more difficult to bring up than Stephen had been, at least as a teenager. But Sara, as expected, didn't budge, saying she was tired of sandbagging, so Janet got up from her chair, inviting Beverly to go outside and help. They left Sara to brood alone.

But within the hour Sara had to give up the living room to Agatha and Linda Schwartzman, who came rushing into the house to say that the fire department was filling her basement with water and her electricity had been disconnected. "I grabbed a change of clothes and called every hotel and motel in the book and they're all full, Miss McGee, so I'm going to spend the night on a couch at the funeral home, but before I go I wanted to check and see if you're all right."

"Of course I'm all right, and you will not sleep on a couch at the funeral home. I have a perfectly good rollaway upstairs. We will put it in the sewing room and you'll have all the privacy you need."

"No, really, Miss McGee." Miss Schwartzman kept protesting as she followed Agatha upstairs to the rollaway and beyond it to the small room that made up the front turret of the house and overlooked the river. It was her mother's sewing room, which hadn't been in use since her mother's death nearly thirty years ago.

"Goodness gracious," said Agatha, pushing open the door and seeing an accumulation of boxes of clothes, linens, curtains, curtain rods, and books blocking her way in.

"No, really, Miss McGee, I'll be perfectly fine in the funeral home. There are no reviewals scheduled, so it will be very private."

"Good lord, do you think I'd want it on my conscience that a neighbor of mine . . . for lack of a bed . . . spent a night in a mortuary? You will please help me get this room ready for you."

And so Linda Schwartzman, her will no match for Agatha's, brought the number of Agatha's house guests to five.

Agatha retired early because it was exhausting to have five people staying under her roof. She also needed a lot of time to change the sheets on Frederick's bed. Lying there, she let her mind range back over the earlier years of her life, as she'd been in the habit of doing almost every day. This evening her mind was on her grandfather McGee. She had his fear of water to thank for her house standing on high ground. When Agatha's father began looking at places on River Street, Grandfather McGee said he'd refuse to move into any house that wasn't higher above water than all the other houses in the neighborhood.

Grandfather McGee, in his old age, came to live with Agatha and her parents in Staggerford. He came a long way—from Dublin—and he was sorry he made the effort. "I've only meself to blame," she remembered him saying more than once. "Me and me lazy brain." Her father, Peter McGee, attorney-at-law, sent for the old widower without realizing how frail he was at sixty-eight. From the enthusiastic sound of his letters from Eire, Grandfather McGee didn't realize it either. He couldn't wait to get out of the dull, drab, dampish city of his birth and plant his feet on American soil. He wrote:

> *Every last manjack my age is either dead or suffering from the disease of the lazy brain. Why Alby O'Toole just yester-night in the pub couldn't remember his dead wife's name—to show you how bad things have got among my friends—and Alby's younger than myself by a good three years.*

From before his sailing until his train pulled into Staggerford, and except for the eleven-day crossing itself from Liverpool, her father and grandfather were in touch practically every day by telephone. But this being 1921, the connections were bad and the cost prohibitive of small talk, so that one's health and the weather weren't even mentioned. This led to great shock on the part of both of them—so her father told Agatha and her mother—when the train arrived in Fargo on an unseasonably cold November evening and the old man was almost knocked over by the icy wind blowing along the station platform, and Peter McGee didn't recognize this emaciated creature as his own father. On the last leg of the journey—it was scarcely eighty miles by rail from Fargo to Staggerford—the old man got the chills and the sweats, and every time he fell asleep he was awakened by a nightmare.

"Oh, the sea, the waves!" he kept repeating for years afterward, awake and asleep. He was evidently reliving a crossing rough enough to remain vividly in his memory for the rest of his life. Every so often, until his death from a cerebral hemorrhage ten years later, he spoke of the crew member who was lost at sea, washed overboard along with a dozen deck chairs and a lifeboat. And he told about the elegant lady from London who died on-board and was buried at sea. "And did I not envy her deliverance!" he declared to Agatha over and over. "I was that sick meself."

And it wasn't only the strenuous voyage that caused her grand-father's regret; it was the fact that the Irish Republic won its inde-pendence about six months after he left home. "Had I known the dastardly British were going to get off our backs in my lifetime, I'd have never left Dublin, Aggie, me lass."

He repeated the same tales again and again, to the point of tire-someness, and Agatha, in her teens, was of an age to listen. Which is to say she was more or less trapped, her mother busy with house-hold chores and her father occupied by his practice of law. Except during school hours it was Agatha, by edict, who became her grand-father's companion. Did he wish to have company on his late after-noon walk downtown to McGee and Haggerty's law office? Why, Agatha would go along with him. Did he want someone to sit with him when her parents went out for the evening? She was always there.

Agatha was blessed with a prodigious memory. Even now she could recall individual evenings spent over her homework as Grandfather, carefully filling his pipe and rocking slowly back and forth in the maple rocker she now kept in her bedroom, ran on and on about Ireland and his leaving it. "Oh, the sea and the waves," he kept repeating. "See that you avoid leaving your snug wee home and going out on the horrible high seas. Promise me now, me lass, will you? At all costs."

Agatha promised. An easy promise to make, home being in the

middle of Minnesota and about as far from any ocean as it was possible to get. All her life she'd remained deathly afraid of boats, and to this day disliked getting wet, even in the tub or shower.

She must have been twelve or thirteen the night he surprised her with a tale she'd never heard before. It was about her father's Cousin Julia, who'd become a family legend. Julia was the daughter of Grandfather's brother Mick.

"Did you know she resided in the States, lass?"

"I know, Father and I went to her funeral in St. Paul."

"Ah, bless you for that. You knew her then."

"No, only as a dead person."

"She was always one to run off and do wild things." Grandfather chuckled. "My earliest memory of her was the night my brother took the belt to her for going into Dublin on the bus."

Agatha remembered her shock at learning that one of her forebears was wild.

"She wasn't as old as you are today, Aggie, and would you believe it, she hopped on the bus that came out to Sandymount from the city. Oh she was a frisky one all right enough. My brother Mick was a hard man. He disowned her, you know, when she came to the States and married an English pagan named Magnuson."

"You mean she died disowned?"

"No, no, Mick was too softhearted to keep up his dislike of anybody, especially his own flesh and blood. I saw the man weep tears of despair when the letter came saying she died."

"What did she die of?"

"I was never told precisely—some hellish contagion that swept over the States a few years ago."

"The influenza," Agatha told him. It was fresh in her mind, because her only brother died of it.

Agatha fell asleep and dreamed that her brother was mowing the lawn in front of their new house on River Street.

SUNDAY

The enormity of her lie about Willoughby didn't fully strike Agatha until she was sitting in St. Isidore's waiting for Palm Sunday mass to begin. Stationed between Janet and Lillian in her accustomed pew near the front and watching the acolyte—Jessica Rathmann, the ten-year-old granddaugher of a former student—light the altar candles, she went back over the events set in motion by her momentous falsehood. She couldn't understand why she felt relieved when the hearse departed Willoughby. And now, seeing Father Healy at the altar, she was overcome with shame. How could she have felt relieved? Compared to this, Friday afternoon's lie—claiming to Linda Schwartzman that she had never regretted the single life—was nothing. In falsifying Dort Holister's identity she had set something dangerous and unstoppable in motion. The first lie had already necessitated a second lie—about Calista being Dort—and would go on spawning other lies for the rest of her life.

Father Healy began his homily with a funny story, but Agatha was too preoccupied to understand the punch line or to pay any attention to the unfamiliar sound of laughter in church, because she realized with horror that she was making sinners out of others as well as herself. Benji Simms, the Wentworths, Samantha Edgerton the Donut Queen, as well as Howard and Calista Holister—all were trapped in her lie. She foresaw each one of them maintaining this falsehood time after time, down through the years.

And yet—she told herself, kneeling at the elevation of the bread and wine—it wasn't for herself that she lied; it was for the good of an entire community. It was possible that Billy and Inga Wentworth would survive for a time with Dort Holister gone, selling gasoline and snacks to motorists traveling north on U.S. Highway 71, but without the post office to draw people to town, their business, like the others, would eventually die. She'd watched it happen in other places. How sad it was to see the crumbling houses and empty store buildings of Hunterstown and Haymarket, both of which were vigorous communities in the early days of the railroad. It was said that Haymarket once claimed, among its six churches, even a Baptist congregation—a rarity in these parts—and Hunterstown had an opera house, five saloons, and a car dealership.

Her fellow parishioners for many years had been following Agatha's lead in receiving the bread and wine, and although she had been absent from mass for months, they were ready to follow her once again. This caused them some confusion today, because it took them a minute to figure out that Agatha wasn't going to Communion. They proceeded leaderless up the aisle, and many of them, passing in front of her on their way back to their pews, actually turned and stared at her, all the while speculating about her sin, she was sure of it.

After mass she told Janet to bring the car around to the sacristy door and she asked Lillian to come with her to see Father Healy. With only a few parishioners left in the still church lingering at their prayers, the two of them climbed the steps of the sanctuary and took a minute to help each other stiffly to their feet after genuflecting under the high crucifix. "Wait here," she instructed Lillian, who plunked herself obediently down on the acolyte's bench. Weaving breathlessly into the sacristy, Agatha decided that another thing she liked about her new pastor was how convincingly he pretended to be glad to see her. Old Father Finn had always looked askance at her approach, or frightened. "Agatha, how nice to see you here," Father Healy said, already shed of his vestments. "I'll take you off my sick-call list."

She closed the door behind her. "Father, this time I've told a whopper."

"Now now, remember what I said about that."

"No, wait till you hear—it's serious." And this was the moment when she realized to her horror that she could not confess her lie to the priest. By telling him the truth, she would force him either to break the seal of confession and tell the world that Dort is dead, or to implicate himself by keeping her secret and thus become, year after year, a sinner at the altar of God. The thought of being trapped in her sin with no recourse, no turning back, condemned for eternity, caused her to hyperventilate. "Lillian," she called with the last of her breath, and she was hurried out to Janet's van. She rode off in the direction of Mercy Hospital, leaving Lillian and Father Healy at the curb.

"Does this happen to her very often?" he asked.

Lillian's reply was a distracted shrug. She was watching the van disappear.

"Do you know what's eating her?"

"No idea . . . she's a funny old bird."

They stopped short of the hospital, since Agatha's breathing was restored, less by her own will power, it seemed, than by Janet's placid nature and by the blessed sunshine beaming down on the wet, chilly streets.

In the hospital neighborhood there was water standing at the curbs to a depth of four or five inches, and a repellent aroma noticed even by Agatha with her impaired sense of smell. "Sewage," said Janet. "I've heard of places where the sewers get flooded and all that stuff comes up and mixes with the water on the ground."

They found crews of sandbaggers working at intervals along

River Street, staying ahead of the rising Badbattle on the near bank, but across the river they could see water inching up the trees of the picnic area known as Pine Grove Park. Janet stopped her van near one such crew, rolled down her window and called to her daughter.

Sara came running over to the van looking refreshed and cheerful, wearing a yellow sweatshirt and jeans. She was breathless with excitement. "You know what we saw go by just a little while ago? Somebody's garage, the whole thing floating along on its roof, pretty as you please. And we watched all the picnic tables across the river get picked up one by one and carried downriver to New Orleans." Having used sandbagging as an excuse to miss mass, she obviously found these tragic sights invigorating.

"Hop in, Sara, we'll go home and have breakfast."

"No, I had breakfast. I'm staying."

"What did you eat?"

"Rolls. There was a bakery truck came around with yummy rolls for us. Oh, and don't drink any water. There's been a car going around with a P.A. system telling everybody the water supply all over town is in danger of getting poisoned."

A shout went up at water's edge and Sara ran back to watch a door go floating by with a cat sitting on it, looking queenly and unperturbed.

Agatha, still afflicted by flood denial, wanted to verify the water problem by phoning William Mulholland, the city clerk, but Janet wisely overruled her and drove directly to Druppers' Grocery for several gallons of bottled water and bags of food.

At home Janet drove up the sloping back yard and parked her van near the door. They found two of Agatha's guests in the kitchen, Linda Schwartzman making coffee and listening to Beverly Cooper's account of her son's mental aberrations.

"One time I had to drive him clear into Atlanta to a hospital 'cuz there wasn't any room for him anywhere else—my husband, my first husband, was stationed in Georgia at the time—and if you don't think that was some awful trip! Over fifty miles of terror, that's what it was. For one thing there was a hurricane going on and I couldn't hardly see where I was going, and for another thing, every time I slowed down, Owen kept opening his door and trying to get out. Hi, Miss McGee, how was church? Here, Janet, let me help you with those bags."

"There's more in the van," Janet said.

As the two of them stepped outside, Agatha hurried into the living room to answer the phone. It was Lillian calling to say that Sunset Home was being evacuated. "Those of us with someplace to go are staying in town, and the rest are being hauled off to higher ground. I told them you'd take me in, Agatha, so I won't get hauled away."

"The more the merrier," said Agatha grimly. "But you'd have to sleep on the living room couch."

"The couch! Agatha, you haven't been upstairs lately, so maybe you forgot, you've got two empty bedrooms up there."

"They're not empty anymore. Every bed in this house is occupied."

"Who . . . ?"

Agatha told her about yesterday's five visitors.

"You mean they stayed overnight?"

"Of course they stayed overnight. They're all displaced by the flood."

Lillian paused, apparently to form a mental picture of where everybody slept. "Well, if Frederick's in Willoughby. I could sleep in his room."

"Sorry, I beat you to it."

"But Agatha, what's wrong with your room downstairs? Your house is high enough to keep you out of the water."

"Dort's using my room, Lillian."

There was silence again on the line. Agatha could sense her old friend fuming. Finally she heard, "I *hate* being hauled out of here—clear to Berrington, they say."

"Lillian, come to your senses. You have a perfectly good house out my back door. Why not stay with Imogene?"

"Oh, Imogene!"

"Well, suit yourself, Lillian. You'd be welcome here, you know that. I simply haven't any space except the couch."

Lillian hung up. Ordinarily Agatha would have called her right back, reprimanding her for poor telephone etiquette, but this morning there was breakfast to see to. Tying on an apron, she wondered about the antagonism between Lillian and her daughter. Her "Oh, Imogene!" was spoken with disgust.

Calista Holister emerged from the downstairs bedroom wearing another flowered dress, but brighter than yesterday's, and looking more cheerful than Agatha expected. She greeted everyone as though for the first time—yesterday's fog had obviously lifted—but when Agatha reintroduced her as Dort, she looked confused. Through half of breakfast she was silent, apparently groping in her mind for the source of her name change. When she finally uncovered yesterday's deception, she turned to Agatha with a self-satisfied nod of her head.

Beverly, having moved her car up next to Janet's, sat down to breakfast and dominated the table talk, continuing her tale of Owen in Atlanta. "I stayed in the city overnight, and when I went to visit him the next day in the hospital, he was in a kind of coma. He'd taken a whole handful of pills when a nurse's back was turned, had tried to kill himself, and do you know what the hospital did about that? They made me take him home. They kicked him out because he wasn't playing fair, they said. That's right, they kicked him out of the hospital. Oh, those stupid assholes, pardon my French. Well, at least they arranged for someplace else to take him in—I'll give them that. It was another hospital across the city in a suburb, and that's where he finally got better. His attitude improved, his spirits started rising, and I think it was because of a fellow named Dan. They became friends from the start. They played pool together. They both got paying jobs on the groundskeeping crew. Dan and Owen were both timid in group, but between them they got so they'd speak up once in a while. Dan knew how to play the five-string guitar but he didn't have one and so I took mine and I left it with him. But Dan couldn't stand being hospitalized. One day he ran away. They found him and brought him back but he ran away a second time and Owen never heard from him again. I'll have to ask Owen what happened to my five-string guitar."

Then Janet joined in with a description of a treatment center her husband Randy Meers was once in—for gambling addiction— and Agatha was astonished at the candor of both of these women. How different from her own younger days. If anyone in the McGee family was in need of treatment—which of course they weren't, everyone she knew being spared all forms of addiction and mental aberration—it would have been kept hush-hush, never spoken of outside the family circle.

"This was in St. Paul," said Janet, "a place as beautiful as a country club. In fact it was called a club, The Erikson Club, and there was this pond outside Randy's window and long, sloping lawns and a putting green and gardens—it was just plain heavenly—but it didn't work. I'm not saying it didn't work for others; I'm just saying it didn't work for Randy and about three other guys who were in there with him. Every day they played a round of golf for money. There's a lot of group therapy at the Erikson Club, and every night after therapy they pulled their chairs up to a table and played poker for high stakes. Not that they exchanged money on the spot—they weren't even allowed to keep any money on them until they were released. No, they kept track on slips of paper and paid each other off when they got out. Randy came home laughing about it. He said they were encouraged to go for walks every morning around the grounds, and these guys would bet how many ducks they'd see on the pond, how many drakes, how many females, how many ducklings. It was worse than no treatment at all, because it made a cynic out of Randy. Say what you will about Randy"—here, she glanced at Agatha who'd never held a high opinion of her husband—"he'd never been cynical."

Linda Schwartzman joined in then, telling them about her former husband Manny, the Ohio undertaker, who could have used a good dose of treatment for his aggravating behavior. "He couldn't stand to be wrong. He was so highhanded that nobody, especially women, could stand being around him. The last straw was when he started bawling out a dead man's widow at his funeral because she wrote poems Manny didn't like. Her name was Mildred Stacy Tibb. She was the self-appointed poet laureate of Mortonson County, and her poems had been appearing in our local newspaper, and every time Manny read one he'd get hot under the collar. Of course they weren't much as poetry; they were sappy and all that, but the minute he figured out who she was, he took her aside from her husband's grave and pointed out all the problems in her poems. I was there. I saw it happen; I was so embarrassed, I can't tell you how embarrassed I was. That was the day I decided to walk."

Agatha saw Calista's expression grow intensely serious. She used to see this look come suddenly into Calista's eyes when she was a girl in the sixth grade. It meant that a thought had occurred to her and she was searching for a way to express it. Agatha called on her—"Yes, what is it?"—as she did fifty years ago.

"I was just thinking, men are so . . ." Calista looked meekly around the table for the right word to describe her brother.

"Awful," said Beverly.

"They can be such problems," said Linda Schwartzman.

"Like women," said Janet Meers, always the fair-minded voice of reason.

Agatha didn't respond. She was thinking of the two men she'd known very well, besides James O'Hannon—her father and her grandfather, both of them stalwart, peerless men. Her father, Peter McGee, a jolly little man and one of Staggerford's first attorneys. She recalled his fatal coronary and worked back through his two terms in the state legislature, his four campaigns for state office (the first and last unsuccessful), and his significant court cases as Staggerford's foremost lawyer. He was a small, red-haired Irishman who came to the States as a young man in the company of his older sister and her husband. The sister died not long after their emigration. Agatha's father had a gregarious, happy nature, and it occurred to her now to wonder why she herself had never come close to resembling her father in personality.

Peter McGee, for being such an outspoken man, was curiously lighthearted. Agatha's mother, on the other hand, was serious and silent. I have inherited Father's outspokenness and Mother's seriousness, she told herself, but I do not have her silent ways nor am I, alas, lighthearted like Father. How was Father able to lay aside his convictions and come home to supper so jolly after spending an hour over his afternoon beer with his political enemies in Hanley's Saloon? I thought it was the Irish who were the grudging race, yet Father was 100 percent Irish and never bore a grudge while I, only seven-eighths—one of Mother's grandparents was English—recall every last wrong ever done to me, and my memories of small schoolgirl slights can still bring me to a boil.

Agatha's mother kept her strong ethical opinions to herself year after year, because, as she told her daughter, "God hates a mouthy woman." By which she almost certainly meant her father instead of God, because Agatha later learned from her mother's two unmarried sisters that her Grandfather Cunningham held god-like sway over the household of their childhood. They were punished a good deal, and for small offenses, such as talking out of turn at dinner. "That is to say," stated Agatha's Aunt Christine when she was very old, "interrupting Daddy when he was speaking."

"Or sometimes," added her sister Louise, "it meant saying a word Daddy didn't care for, like 'garbage' or 'smut.' Daddy had the most sensitive ear for language, an almost pathological love-hate relationship with it. There was nothing he liked better than a well-turned speech. Why, remember, Christine, on the Fourth of July he'd stand under the hot sun for hours in order to hear the speakers."

"Till the last dog was hung and the flags were taken down," said Aunt Christine, smiling at the memory.

As a girl Agatha loved hearing these two women talk. They lived a kind of symbiotic life in the apartment they shared in St. Paul, and the way they could talk a subject to death convinced the young Agatha that they weren't the brainiest people God created, but every time she was in their company she did her utmost to get them started. She was particularly interested to hear them on the subject of their father because Agatha, with her own pathological relationship with language, was so amused to hear this pair of arthritic and ancient ladies refer to their father as Daddy.

At noon the five women were standing at the front window watching the water continue to rise when Agatha sensed another presence in the room. She turned and found that they had been joined by her neighbor from across the alley.

"Imogene!" She was shocked to see this unfriendly woman who hadn't paid her a call in years standing there in her military raincoat. Then, noticing the duffel bag she'd brought with her, as well as the look of desperation in her eyes, she understood. "You poor thing, you've been flooded out of your house."

Imogene nodded curtly. "Water's coming up in the basement."

"Well, I have only one flat surface for sleeping left in the house. This couch. But you're welcome to it."

Imogene took immediate possession of the couch by sitting on it, in her coat, with her duffel bag at her side. She looked at Agatha accusingly. "I thought you said we wouldn't have a flood."

"It seems I was wrong." This being a difficult thing for Agatha to admit, she quickly introduced her other guests. "This is Beverly, whom you may remember, a friend from years ago. And this is our new neighbor, Linda Schwartzman. You know Janet. And surely you know Dort Holister from Willoughby."

Although she was greeted by all four of the women, Imogene ignored three of them and centered her attention on Linda Schwartzman. "You're the undertaker lady."

Linda gently corrected her. "A funeral director who happens to be female." Then she added, "I have water in my cellar, too."

Agatha climbed the stairs to Frederick's bedroom, leaving the two of them discussing the depth of water in their basements. Janet turned Calista and Beverly's attention back outside by pointing out her daughter in the yellow sweatshirt working among the sandbaggers.

What a lot I've done already and it's barely one o'clock, thought Agatha proudly as she lay down on the bed and covered herself with the orange and chartreuse afghan Lillian had given her years ago. Early mass followed by four guests for breakfast. I haven't been this active since. . . . She fell asleep in the act of lowering her head to the pillow.

It was a scream that woke her, a bloodcurdling noise from the bottom of the stairs, followed by a woman's voice saying, "Where's

Agatha? She'll settle this." It sounded like Lillian, but it couldn't be—Lillian had been trucked off to Berrington and higher ground. Agatha had thrown off the afghan and was sitting on the edge of the bed collecting herself when she heard someone coming up the stairs—a slow ascent remindful of Lillian's plodding footsteps.

"Agatha, there you are, and I'm at my wits' end." It *was* Lillian, standing in the bedroom doorway, still in her coat and kerchief, holding a grocery bag and fanning her red face with her free hand. "You gave your couch to Imogene and now I have no place to sleep."

"But I thought you went to Berrington."

"If only I did. No, I decided to stay here in case you needed help."

Agatha knew this to be the whole truth and not a play on her sympathy, for dear Lillian, like Beverly, was incapable of guile or pretense. Getting to her feet, she said, "Well, the other side of this bed hasn't been spoken for."

Lillian stepped into the room then, set her bag on the bed, and took out a nightgown, which she slipped under one of the pillows. She placed her toothbrush and a couple of pill bottles on Frederick's dresser.

"I thought I heard a scream downstairs," said Agatha. "I must have dreamed it."

"That was no dream; that was my daughter when I said I'd come to sleep on your couch. Imogene's touchy as a cat these days. It happens every year around her birthday."

"Let's see," Agatha calculated. "You were thirty when she was born. This would be only her fiftieth."

"She used to love her birthdays, but all that changed when she lost her dad. Ever since Lyle died, she's hated to get older. Between you and me, I think she's scared of death."

"Aren't we all," said Agatha, suddenly reminded of yesterday's lie and the threat of eternal punishment.

"What's to be scared of? You, Agatha—are you scared? You of all people will be sitting up there at God's right hand, I'm sure of that."

Agatha mumbled, "I am heartily sorry."

"What's that?" asked Lillian.

"I'll be down in a minute." She shut Lillian out of the room and, going to her knees at the side of the bed, started the Act of Contrition over again. "Oh my God, I am heartily sorry for having offended Thee . . ."

Downstairs she found Lillian and Imogene bickering in the living room ("Mother, will you please shut up and listen!"), and Sara Meers, her dark mood restored to her, lying on the loveseat in the sunroom with the cell phone to her ear. ("We saw this totally cool, off-the-shoulder prom dress in a catalog, but my old-fashioned mom said it's immodest and besides it costs too much.") She went to her bedroom and found Calista napping. The other three women were huddled over the kitchen table, evidently discussing a secret, because they stopped talking as soon as Agatha entered.

"Pardon me," she said, "I thought I'd make a pot of tea."

Their silence was irritating.

"Well, don't let me interfere, I can come back later."

"All right, Agatha, we *were* talking about you," Janet confessed. "We were saying how you don't look the least bit sick."

"Is that so remarkable? Who says I'm sick?"

"It was in the *Weekly*."

"Oh that rag. You can't believe a thing it says. The publisher drinks and the editor's a stranger in town." She regulated the flame under the teakettle. "I'd like to know who's been telling tales about my health."

She'd also like to know what had happened between Lillian and her daughter, because the swinging door opened suddenly and into the kitchen strode Lillian, followed by her daughter, who was telling her to lighten up. "Your trouble is you've never known how to relax."

"Relax! Who's the uptight one in this family? It sure isn't me."

Agatha was astonished at the fire in Lillian's voice. She'd never seen her old friend, who'd spent a lifetime being docile as a sheep, so angry.

Imogene didn't let up. "Listen, you know what your trouble is? You never read any of the self-help books I bring you. You sit there knitting all day, thinking up mean things to say to me."

Her mother turned and glared at her. "Shame on you, for fighting in Agatha's house."

"Shame on *me*! Me? You started it. You're the one who came in and plunked yourself on the couch like you owned it. You're the one—"

"Come here, both of you," said Agatha, opening the door and stepping out into the chilly back porch. "I have something to show you." Lillian and Imogene followed her. Agatha pointed to the far corner, and when they took a step in that direction, she came back inside and, closing the door, said, "Let me know when you can be civil and I'll let you in." She turned the key in the lock.

There was a moment of stunned silence on both sides of the door, before Linda Schwartzman asked, with trepidation, "Are they always like that?"

Janet told her, "It's typical of Imogene, but not of her mother."

They heard the outer door open and close, then a gentle rapping on the kitchen door. "Yes?" said Agatha.

Lillian called out, "At least let *me* back in, Agatha. I've cooled down."

"What about Imogene?"

"She left."

Lillian entered, apparently unembarrassed, and went directly to the stove to take over the tea making. "I hope you've put in a lot of groceries," she said, "because from the looks of things we're going to be here for a while."

Agatha told her not to worry. "Janet went shopping on our way home from church."

"I probably should go again," said Janet. "We didn't buy enough for eight people."

"You're too late," said Lillian. "Downtown's all closed off. I just came through. There's water in the streets."

Sara came into the room to say she was hungry, followed by Imogene (who'd reentered the house through the front door), asking, "What's for dinner?"

"Chicken and dressing," said Janet, going to the refrigerator.

Agatha was shooed out of the kitchen, along with Sara and Imogene, but rather than join these two spoiled daughters in the living room she went again to her bedroom to look in on Calista, who had risen from the bed and was sitting at the dressing table staring into the mirror. It was obvious from her slump-shouldered posture that she was at low ebb. She turned to tell Agatha, "I can't stop crying. Every time I think of Dort lying dead on the stoop, I lose control of myself. What will I do without her, Agatha? How can I go on pretending I'm her? How can I go on alone, living with Howard?"

"Of course you can do those things. Just get a hold of yourself. You're stronger than you think." Agatha revealed none of the sympathy she felt for this poor, bereft woman, none of the doubt. Was saving the economy of Willoughby worth putting Calista through all this trouble? Whenever she felt the need of a model of fortitude, Agatha was in the habit of bringing Abraham Lincoln to mind. All her life she had wondered if saving the Union was worth the hundreds of thousands of lives that were lost, and yet Lincoln seemed never to have had a moment's doubt. "Frederick can go to full time and help you out in the post office. Everything will be fine, Calista.

Whenever you have a weak moment, go to your room and get over it."

Calista wiped away her tears. "But Howie can be so ugly with me sometimes. There isn't a bit of softness about him."

"Think about how your sister handled him all these years." Agatha took her hand in her own. "You're Dort now, so do what Dort did."

"But Dort was stronger than I am."

"Not anymore, she isn't." She gave the hand a gentle pat and left the room.

Dinner was sumptuous and eaten in the dining room, Agatha at the head of the table, with Beverly and Janet on her right and left. Again Beverly brought up her son's schizophrenia, a topic Agatha immediately squelched by covering her hand with her own and saying, "First we'll say grace. And then we'll spend a few minutes . . . on something more edifying than mental illness."

Beverly won Janet's heart by easily acceding to Agatha's wishes. Here's a woman who understands Agatha the way I do, thought Janet. She conformed to Agatha's wishes, it seemed, as much out of respect for Agatha's wisdom as for her age.

Table talk was directionless and breezy at first, everyone unwilling to bring up a subject that might not qualify as edifying. Then Janet, considering herself and Beverly, said, "Do you ever wonder why some people hit it off right away while others never seem to entirely get along?"

"Of course," said Agatha. "It's been one of the mysteries of my career. Why do some students have an affinity for one another while others don't. I used to think it was matching intelligence that drew them together. Or matching interests. But I know from my own experience that it's neither of those." She was thinking of the enduring bonds between herself and Frederick, herself and Lillian. Neither of them was quick of mind or drawn to her interests, she thought. And then, frowning intensely, she suddenly blurted, "What are my interests?" Until this winter she read two or three books each month. After St. Isidore's closed, she would drop in at the public school just to smell education going on. She never was much of a joiner, but she did serve as bookkeeper for the northern Minnesota chapter of Habitat for Humanity. Now nothing seemed quite so pressing as her afternoon nap.

Linda Schwartzman agreed with Agatha's assessment of friendship, recounting the experiences of girls she'd known, growing up in northern Minnesota. She said she had an older cousin, a girl named Libby Girard who fell in love with a boy who became a Catholic priest. "They might have been of equal intelligence," said Linda, "but she wasn't the least bit interested in religion. He was a very handsome boy, but it had to be something more than looks, because I don't think she's gotten over him to this day. I understand they still see each other. His name is Frank Healy."

Janet shot a look at Agatha, to see if this news about their pastor alarmed her, which it evidently did because she found Agatha's eyes fastened coldly on her own. Next, she glanced at Lillian and Calista, the other two churchgoing Catholics at this table, but neither of them seemed to have been paying attention. It was Imogene who was most excited by the thought of the local priest's involvement with a woman. She broke out in a harsh, convulsive laugh that kept recurring at intervals throughout the meal.

Agatha steered the talk around this unedifying news and back to her diminishing interests. "You know, the older I get, the fewer things interest me in life. Is that natural, I wonder? Imogene knows I hardly ever check a book out of the library anymore. And I've let my two or three magazine subscriptions lapse. Why, I wouldn't even see the *Staggerford Weekly* if Frederick didn't bring it home every Thursday."

Calista concurred, speaking up for the first time. "My sister used to tell me I had the narrowest interests she'd ever seen. She used to say the only thing I cared about is what happened in front of the post office." Tears sprang into her eyes, but she bore up. "Like you, Agatha, I got that way after I quit reading, only I quit long before you did." She emitted a little laugh. "I quit reading the day I graduated from high school."

Lillian had the solution to this problem. "*The National Enquirer's* what keeps me interested in things. Why just this winter, do you know how many husbands Elizabeth Taylor's been married to? Eight. I had no idea. I thought it was about six. And her weight's been up and down something horrible over these last years. You see one picture of her she looks fine, and the next she looks like a cow."

"Mother!" said Imogene, by which she meant, Don't display your ignorance.

"Tut!" said her mother, by which she meant, Never mind. She explained to the others, "My daughter's mad because the library board won't let her have a subscription to it. I tell her she could increase library traffic by at least half again as much by putting *The National Enquirer* on display—you know it costs us an arm and a leg to subscribe to at the Sunset Home—but the library board put the kibosh on that idea."

Imogene cleared her throat as preamble to a pronouncement: "It's possible to have too many interests in life."

Beverly was quick to agree. "It seems like if I added one more interest to my life I'd collapse under the load."

"I don't agree at all," said Linda Schwartzman, addressing Imogene. "You can't have too many interests."

"Oh yes, you can," said Beverly. "I'm pulled in too many directions already, and now with Owen taking so much of my time . . ."

"But don't you see," Linda insisted, "your son, besides being an interest in your life, is a huge problem in your life. It's crowding out everything else. Once you solve your son's problem, you won't feel so put upon. You'll have room in your life for other things."

"She can't solve his problem," said Imogene. "He has to solve his own problem."

Linda shrugged. "Yes, well, whatever."

Another pronouncement. "In cases of addiction, it's the addicted person who has to come to terms with . . ."

Janet interrupted, wrenching the conversation back to where it started. "Agatha, you claim not to have many interests, but I see seven of them sitting around this table. You'll never lose your interest in people."

Her daughter, Sara, spoke up for the first time to ask, "Can I have more chicken?"

"Sorry," said Janet, "no second helpings today. We're saving the rest for another meal."

"Curb your appetite, young woman," warned Imogene. "Children nowadays are much too fat for their own good. It's from French fries and hamburgers day after day. I see them in the library after school, fat, stupid things, asking me to find books that are right in front of their noses. Follow my example; I've never been an ounce overweight, have I, Mother? My weight has always been ideal for my height, which is five-six."

"Stop bragging," said her mother.

Assuming every teenager to be as stupid as those who frequented her library, Imogene added, in aid of Sara, "That's five feet, six inches."

In the evening William Mulholland called from city hall, checking on Agatha. "It looks like our temporary dikes along River Street aren't going to be high enough, Miss McGee. Your place is going to be surrounded by water for another forty-eight hours."

She covered the mouthpiece and told Calista, Lillian, and Beverly, who were sitting with her in the living room. "It's the city clerk, predicting disaster." Her wry smile told them not to worry. She glanced outside, but it was too dark to see anything.

She put the phone back to her ear and heard, "We can come now and pick you up and take you to one of our shelters."

"Thank you, William, I wouldn't think of leaving."

"All your neighbors have cleared out. You've got your choice of the high school gym or the Congregational Church."

"No, no, William, we'll be just fine as we are. Remember, I am on higher ground than my neighbors. My grandfather was afraid of a flood, you see . . . and he prevailed upon my father to buy the highest house along River Street."

"Well okay, if that's your final decision . . . it's possible, though it isn't likely, that you'll have to move up to the second floor."

"Don't be ridiculous. We're safe as can be."

"You've got French there with you?"

"Frederick's in Willoughby."

"Who's 'we' then?"

"Friends and neighbors. Let's see, there are six, seven, eight of us altogether."

"Eight. Jeez, you're going to need a lot of food for eight people."

"Oh, I know. I have some canned goods stored in the basement. And I made a lot of chokecherry jam last fall. Lillian Kite bakes the best bread." A wave of warmth and exhilaration washed over her. "Isn't it exciting, Willian?" She felt giddy, the way she felt at pajama parties seventy years ago.

"Have you got flour, Miss McGee?"

"Flowers? Of course not. It's only April."

"Flour, for baking bread."

"Oh, yes, plenty. But it's much too early for flowers, William. Surely you must know that."

"How about beds. Have you got places for eight people to sleep?"

"Oh, yes, when my father bought this house, everyone wanted to know . . . why he needed all this room. He told them he expected company. He was a great one for company, my father. Why, we had the archbishop stay with us one time. And Governor Gunderson before he became governor. And others too numerous—"

"The reason I ask, we can drop off army cots if you need them."

"Well, a cot would be appreciated actually. Then Lillian and I won't have to share a bed."

"Now, you'll have to give me the names of all eight, Miss McGee. We don't want anybody to go missing. Lillian Kite is there, is she?"

"Lillian and her daughter Imogene. They aren't getting along at all well. I don't know what's at the bottom of it." There was a time when Agatha would have held back this information as too private to spread outside the family, but her sense of family had broadened in recent years to include a good many of her former students.

"Yes, and who else."

"Dort Hollister is here from Willoughby. Her sister Calista died yesterday."

"Yes, sorry. A friend of yours, I suppose."

Oh, dear, word was out. There was no turning back the deception now. "We go way back. All three Holisters were students of mine nearly fifty years ago. They've had the Willoughby post office, let's see . . . Dort, how long have you had the post office?"

"Miss McGee, if you don't mind, I've got a lot of people to call."

"Fourteen years; think of it."

"Who else is there?"

"Janet Meers is here, with her daughter, Sara. Her son, Stephen, is stranded in their house on the river. There's no telling where her husband is. Linda Schwartzman is here."

"Schwartzman, how is that spelled?"

She spelled it for him.

"That's the new lady undertaker, isn't it?"

"A funeral director who happens to be a woman . . . is a better way to say it, William."

"*Weekly* says she's from out of state. Tell her she's got thirty days to get a Minnesota driver's license."

"And Beverly Cooper is here. You will remember her as your high school classmate . . . Beverly Bingham."

"Beverly Bingham, holy jeez, Miss McGee, would you know her home address? I"m trying to get our class together for a reunion this summer."

"I'll put her on the phone."

"No, not now, I"m too busy. Have her call me later. All right, who else is there?"

"That's it, William."

"But that's only seven names."

"I am number eight."

"Of course, sorry."

"You're much too young to be so forgetful, William."

"Silly mistake, Miss McGee. Good-bye."

"But you're asking if my flowers are up in April. That's not a good sign."

"Good-bye."

Agatha reported to her guests, "He says we're in for the flood's lasting another forty-eight hours. Which means we can get rid of some of my canned goods in the basement. Lillian, he's going to drop off an army cot for you to sleep on. And Beverly, he wants you to phone him and give him your address. It seem there's a class reunion in the offing."

She went to the kitchen where Linda Schwartzman was helping Janet put supper together and Imogene was sitting at the table paging through a magazine. The excitement she felt on the phone was still with her. She couldn't contain it. She sat at the table and said, "I have a party sort of feeling that I haven't felt since I was a girl . . . when three or four of my friends would come and stay overnight. Your mother was always one of them," she told Imogene, who didn't raise her eyes from the page she was examining. "And Mary Felton, usually, and Mary Adamson, and Mary Ann Thelen. Think of it, three Marys in the neighborhood . . . actually four, counting my mother, and now there hasn't been a Mary baptized at St. Isidore's in years. Every baby girl brought into the world is now named Jessica. And every boy is named either Joshua or Trevor. What are you two preparing?"

"We decided to make chicken salad," said Janet. "To make the last of the chicken go farther."

"The *last* of it? But you said you bought two chickens this morning."

Janet shrugged. "Eight hungry people."

Eating supper, surrounded by her seven guests, she was warmed by the feeling of pajama-party exuberance that had overtaken her.

After supper they took up the indelicate matter of what to do about the lack of water in the toilets. By rummaging through closets, Agatha found two covered chamber pots that hadn't been in use since before her parents died. These she assigned to Calista and Lillian and specified that they be emptied each morning into one of the five-gallon pails in the back porch. "The rest of you will use covered coffee cans, which I have been saving in the basement for years." Claiming that her eyes were too weak to see in the dimly lit basement, she sent Janet down. This was only partly a fib because the light really was dim, but what she truly feared was seeing water trickling into her cellar. Janet, however, returning with half a dozen of the more than forty empty cans that occupied most of the shelving, reported that no water was to be seen. That was when the electricity went off.

They all gathered in the living room then and were listening by candlelight to Beverly's comparison of the various psych wards her son had been admitted to, when they heard the sound of heavy footsteps on the front porch and a knock at the door. Janet went to answer it and found a man in waders offering them an army cot.

"Yes, tell him it's needed," called Agatha from her chair. "Is that you, William?"

"Nielsen, ma'am, Jack Nielsen," he shouted into the room. "We met the other day in Druppers' Grocery." He added something she didn't catch.

"You'll have to speak up so I can hear you."

Janet conveyed his message. "He's the new butcher at Druppers'."

"Can't he step in where I can see him?"

"I've got my boots on, ma'am. I'd get your carpet all wet."

"Well, take them off, for heaven's sake."

"Can't do that, ma'am. Nothing underneath but my underwear."

The word "underwear" caused Imogene, on the couch, to snort with disgusted laughter.

"He's wearing waders," Janet explained, setting the folded-up cot at the foot of the stairs.

"Good-bye, ma'am, I gotta get going. My buddy's waiting."

"Just a minute, Mr. Nielsen, there's something I need to ask you."

He waited patiently for her to come to the door and peer out at him. He was a short man holding a flashlight and dressed in rubber up to his chest.

"I didn't see you drive up," she said. "Where are you parked?"

"We're parked down there." He stood aside and beamed his flashlight on a man halfway down the steps to the street. The man,

facing away from the house, appeared to be sitting down and grip-
ping, with both hands, the railing beside the steps.

"Why, he's sitting in a boat," she exclaimed.

"That's right, ma'am, that's my fishing boat," he said proudly.
"I volunteered it for service during the flood. Oh, and by the way,
Mr. Mulholland told me to tell you if you need anything, just call
him up right away. The phones in this part of town are going dead
in about half an hour. G'night now, ma'am."

There was the sound of an outboard motor starting, and as the
boat purred off into the night, Agatha and her guests carried a can-
dle each to the four corners of the house, looked out four windows,
and saw moonlit water in all directions. Her house was an island.

MONDAY

Morning dawned still and clear, full of birdsong. Looking down from French's bedroom, Agatha found that the water had crept up to within ten or twelve feet of her house. In a moment of vertigo, she seemed to be looking down from the bridge of a ship. Lillian, getting out of the other side of the bed (the cot proved too creaky and uncomfortable), joined her at the window and pointed at her back door across the alley, where the water stood higher than the threshold. This elicited from Lillian nothing more than a sigh, and she went back to bed.

Agatha, captain of the ship, was awake for the day. She quickly dressed and went downstairs. Imogene, too, was up and dressed. She was sitting in Agatha's chair by the window, and, for once in her life, she looked cowed, overcome, afraid.

"Well, well," said Agatha, laying a hand on her shoulder and shuddering as she looked out at the water extending from her porch steps to beyond the park on the far bank of the river. Trees and branches of trees as well as somebody's garbage can were carried along on the current. Imogene was trembling.

"What's the matter, Imogene? Are you worried about the library?"

"Where am I going to live, Agatha? I looked out your back porch at my house and the water's up to the first floor. I've got no place . . ." She averted her face, wiping away a tear.

"I thought you were buying a condominium."

"I've been *thinking* of buying one."

"Well, I'm sure there are rooms for rent. Motels if nothing else."

Imogene stamped her foot, crying, "I don't *want* a room, I want a condo!"

Their conversation woke Calista who came out in her robe and slippers, looking haggard. Agatha apologized. "Sorry to wake you so early, Dort. Go back to bed. The sun isn't quite up yet."

Gazing out at the water Calista paid her no attention. "My sister, Agatha. We can't have her funeral until the water goes down." Her eyes filled with tears.

"That's not our worry. Let Linda Schwartzman and Father Healy figure it out."

"But what if the cemetery is under water?"

"It can't be under water, Dort. It's a hilltop cemetery."

"Oh," she said tremulously, "you're right."

Imogene interrupted her fretting to state, "The Staggerford cemetery is the highest point in Berrington County."

"She'll be buried in Willoughby," Agatha told her. She left those two weepy women, and went to the kitchen, wondering, not for the first time, if Calista could carry off the deception. If she couldn't, Agatha realized with shame, her lie would be revealed to all the world.

She was about to fill her coffeemaker with water when she was reminded by the stopped clock over the stove that there was no electricity, no running water. "Well, let them drink tea," she murmured to herself, setting her half-filled kettle on the stove, but she discovered that her gas burners didn't work. Worse than that, she despaired when she found herself down to her last teabag. How could this be? She'd never in her life run out of tea. Then she remembered—tea was an item on Friday's misplaced grocery list. Instead of making a second trip to the store, Frederick had driven her to Willoughby to visit the Holisters.

She returned to the living room to phone William Mulholland. She couldn't get a dial tone. "No telephone service," Imogene told her.

The sheriff's water-patrol boat went speeding downstream, and Agatha, swept by a wave of panic, went out onto her porch to flag him down, but she was too late. She lingered there in the warmth of the rising sun. At least the warmth was a blessing because without electricity her furnace wouldn't start. Standing on the porch, she was struck by the silence, the stillness. No traffic. No neighbors. Just the small gurgling sounds of moving water. But it didn't seem to be moving fast enough. How long would her house be an island? Days? A week? She had lost her courage, her confidence. She pictured herself and her seven guests, whenever the water receded, discovered dead of starvation.

As soon as everyone was gathered in the kitchen eating corn flakes and the last of the milk, she announced their predicament. With a steadiness of voice that surprised even herself—her voice from the classroom—she said, "We're in a pickle, my friends. Electricity isn't our only problem. We're running out of food. And since the telephone doesn't work we're completely stranded. There's no telling when William Mulholland will come around. Are there any questions or suggestions?"

"The phone's no problem," said Janet. "We can use Sara's cell phone." She sent her daughter upstairs for it.

Calista meanwhile consulted with Linda Schwartzman concerning the funeral. Although Calista didn't say so, Linda sensed that her biggest worry was the condition of the body. "Don't worry," Linda assured her. "I've put your sister on ice."

Sara returned with the phone. "Who do you want to call first, Agatha? I'll dial it."

"Will that little thing reach Willoughby?" she asked, not entirely convinced of the phone's reliability.

"Sure. You can call France if you want to."

"I think we should check on Frederick and Howard first. What's your number at the post office, Dort?"

Calista told Sara, who punched in the numbers and handed the phone to Agatha. Frederick answered on the first ring.

"Frederick, how are you getting along?"

"Okay."

"How is Howard?"

"Howie's okay. How are you?" Frederick's voice grew suddenly very weak.

"We're fine, except we're running out of food. Has the water receded?"

"Yeah, it's gone down quite a bit. We figure we'll be able to go out on part of the route day after tom . . ."

The phone went dead. Janet took it and asked Sara what the problem was.

"It's out of power," said Sara. "It needs to be plugged in."

"You have the transformer?"

"Sure."

"Well, go and plug it in. You should have plugged it in overnight."

Sara drew herself up in her most imperious pose and said with disdain, "There is no electricity, remember, Mother?"

Which accounted for the atmosphere of dread that pervaded the house for the rest of the day. No one spoke of it, but Agatha could sense that the possibility of death by starvation was at the back of everyone's mind.

Everyone, that was, except Lillian who sat knitting as placidly as she'd been doing for years—*click, click, clickety click*—listening to the conversations around her and not listening as her thoughts strayed far away, murmuring now and then her agreement or mild disagreement, seldom taking her eyes from her needles and yarn. Today she was thinking how remarkably talkative women were. Ever since she arrived yesterday, Agatha's house, normally silent, had been ringing with female conversations. Lillian herself seldom took part. Twenty years married to Lyle Kite cured her of idle talk. Lyle was the quietest man she had ever met. He'd come home from work—he was a park ranger—and take off his shoes and read the paper through supper and then listen to the radio till bedtime. It was unbelievable how you could miss a man like that. When Lyle died she was beside herself with grief, although, following his example, she tried not to let it show—Lyle never displayed emotion of any kind. It wasn't until she started reading that she found relief. For years she'd been resisting Imogene's scolding her for not reading, but that was because she wasn't yet familiar with *The National Enquirer*. The goat boy of Tuscany, the divorces and couplings of movie stars, the truth about the Roswell aliens—there was something fascinating on every page of every issue. Now she was starved for it. She'd let Agatha talk her into giving up *The National Enquirer* for Lent. Five weeks without it and one week to go. She wasn't sure she could make it to Easter Sunday.

The very sight of Lillian in her chair across the room had a calming effect on Agatha, who was grateful for her imperturbability. If only Imogene possessed a fraction of her mother's composure. By midafternoon Imogene seemed to have alienated everyone but Sara with her whining and complaining. She attached herself to each woman in turn, beginning with Calista, who retreated to her bedroom, and then Beverly, who gave her nearly an hour of sympathy before turning her over to Linda Schwartzman, who tried consoling her with kind words until she figured out that Imogene didn't want consolation but merely an opportunity to watch her listener wilt under her oppressive bitterness and discouragement. After Linda Schwartzman eluded her, Imogene turned to Janet, who, having no more patience with her, turned her over to her sixteen-year-old daughter, who proved to be, much to her surprise, a kindred spirit. The two of them now sat side by side on the couch, agreeing in subdued and sour tones about the awful unfairness of life. From her chair by the window, keeping watch for the sheriff's boat to make a return pass on its way back downtown, and trying to determine if the flood had reached its peak and begun to subside, Agatha heard Sara and Imogene take up the names of their acquaintances one by one and label them creeps, jerks, dolts, and morons.

It was hard to tell if the flood was actually receding or only appeared to be, because a northeast wind had sprung up and disturbed the water, causing waves to lap at the bottom step leading up to the porch. Unworthy as she was, having promulgated the biggest lie she'd ever heard of, Agatha closed her eyes momentarily to say a prayer of thanksgiving to the Lord for providing her with these seven houseguests. They were a powerful distraction from the enormous disaster outside her window and from the monstrous sin she carried in her heart.

Calista, up from a long nap, sat opposite her in Father Healy's chair, silently staring outside in a distracted way. Janet and Beverly, having gone into the basement for the two or three jars of what remained of Agatha's canned vegetables, were in the kitchen stirring together something for supper. Linda Schwartzman was in the sunroom reading Agatha's copy of *The Adventures of Huckleberry Finn*. Agatha couldn't imagine being stranded in her house alone. She would have been crazy with fear. She'd have been camped on her porch shouting at the top of her small voice to the passing boats as she did this morning, and to no avail.

. . .

For the sixth or eighth time today, Agatha saw a boat rounding the bend upstream but, unlike the others, instead of keeping well out from what used to be the riverbank, this one appeared to be headed straight for her house. As it drew closer she saw that it contained two men. She prayed that one of them would be William Mulholland. Sara and Imogene were drawn to the window by the increasing noise of the outboard motor. Linda Schwartzman came in from the sunroom. The boat pulled up to the porch steps and stopped. The man in front tied a rope to the post at the base of the railing.

"Why, it's Howie," said Calista, lifting Dort's glasses off her face and squinting.

This drew Lillian to the window, trailing her yarn. "Howie and Frederick," she said, and started for the door to welcome them, but Sara and Imogene beat her to it.

Agatha watched the two men hand heavy plastic grocery bags to the two women, and then watched Frederick, bless his heart, step out of the boat and steady it for Howard to do the same.

Frederick removed his shoes in the entryway and came in to announce that the food came from Billy and Inga's Jiffystop Station in Willoughby. "God *damn!*" said Imogene, throwing her arms around his neck as Linda Schwartzman shook his hand. Janet came in from the kitchen and embraced him as well, saying, "You're a lifesaver, Fredriko."

"Bless you, bless you," said Agatha, leaving her chair and bending him down to her level in order to kiss his cheek. "You came all the way from Willoughby in a boat?"

"Yep," he told her, nodding rather proudly. "Howie's fishing boat."

"Why, that's eight miles by road. It must be at least twice that by river."

"We figure twenty. Took us an hour and a quarter."

"Well, come in and have supper with us. Where's Howard?"

"There he is," said Calista, pointing to her brother on the porch. He was grinning at them through the front window.

"He won't come in," said Frederick.

"He doesn't like to go into other people's houses," explained his sister. "He's funny that way."

"Tell us news," said Imogene. "Is the water going down?"

"It's going down in Willoughby. We'll get our electricity back tomorrow sometime. They figure you've got another day and a half of high water in Staggerford."

"Not any higher than this, surely," said Agatha hopefully.

"Nope, they say it's as high as it's going to get."

"Who's they?" asked Imogene.

"We've been listening to the weatherpeople on KRKU."

"How?" asked Agatha. "You don't have electricity."

"Howie's got a transistor. It doesn't get much, but it pulls in Rookery."

She turned to Sara. "Do you have a transistor?"

Sara shook her head. Her collection of electronics—computer, cell phone, tape recorder—didn't include a radio.

"We'll leave you Howie's," said Frederick, stepping out onto the porch in his stocking feet and drawing Howie away from the window. Evidently Howie was reluctant to part with the radio, because it took Frederick a full minute to return and present it to Agatha. "Twelve-sixty on the dial," he told her. It was scarcely bigger than the palm of her hand. She handed it to Sara, who switched it on and found KRKU—a string version of "Embraceable You," sounding high-pitched and tinny through the little speaker.

"That's their sign-off piece," said Janet. "KRKU signs off at sundown."

"Well, we can listen tomorrow," said Agatha. "Surely you will stay and eat with us, Frederick."

"Probably have to stay the night. I don't think we can make it back before dark." Seeing a troubled look on several faces, including Agatha's, he added, "Howie can sleep in my bed; I'll take the couch." Apparently this arrangement brought no relief to anyone, so he said, "Just a minute, I'll talk it over with Howie," and he returned once again to the porch.

In his absence Janet offered, "They can have our bed. Sara and I will sleep in the sunroom."

"There's no bed in the sunroom," Agatha reminded her. "Only the loveseat and that's much too short for either of you."

"No, you have scads of extra blankets—we'll sleep on the floor."

"Motherrrrrr," whined Sara, looking betrayed.

"Nonsense, the men can have the sunroom," declared Agatha. "One of them can have the army cot. The other will have to sleep on the floor."

Imogene told Linda Schwartzman confidentially, "If Frederick takes the couch, it won't be the first time we slept together."

"Really?" asked Linda.

Her answer was Imogene's ear-piercing shriek of laughter.

Frederick returned to say it would be impossible to get back to Willoughby in daylight. "It's upstream and the wind's against us. I don't know the river well enough to make it in the dark."

Agatha sent him upstairs for the cot. While he was gone, the front door opened and Howie edged into the entryway. He peeked at the roomful of women.

"Ignore," ordered Agatha, and everyone did so except Calista, who took a step in his direction, and he fled back onto the porch.

It was Frederick who finally drew him indoors to stay, teasing him through the living room and dining room and into the kitchen with the promise of salami sandwiches and potato chips by candlelight.

"Thanks for the invite," said Howie to Agatha as he stepped

through the kitchen doorway, and she unwisely—a teacher's instinct—corrected him: "The word is invitation, Howard."

This set him off once again on his pet peeve—big words—and this time, self-conscious in a roomful of unfamiliar women, he grew more repellently forceful than usual. "Invitation! Dang it, don't come at me with them long words when a perfectly good short word will do!" Agatha slipped away to tend to Calista, who hadn't joined the group in the kitchen. Sizing up his audience, Howie decided that Beverly appeared less threatening than the others, and between mouthfuls of his sandwich he addressed the rest of his remarks to her. "It makes me so dang mad! Who the heck don't understand what 'Thanks for the invite' means? I said to Miss McGee, 'Thanks for the invite,' and she came back at me with a bigger word meaning the same dang thing."

Frederick, meanwhile, avoiding Imogene, who kept giving him flirtatious looks, placed himself between Lillian and Janet and made small talk—a skill it took him years to learn but at which, after five hundred afternoons in Kruger's pool hall, he'd become fairly adept. He began with matters of health and weather and went on to news he'd gathered from Kruger's and the weekly paper. Who was back from wintering in the South. Who stood to profit when the government bought up land for the new stretch of U.S. Highway 71. The unfortunate effect on local business when the highway bypassed town.

Beverly soon tired of Howie's crazy recital and turned her attention to Linda Schwartzman sitting nearby. "So what do you think of Staggerford?"

"Awfully wet." Linda laughed. "No, I'm kidding—it's too early to tell. I've been in town less than a week."

"Well, this is one way to get acquainted then."

Linda nodded, looking around at her housemates. Two rural

mail carriers, a realtor's wife, an elderly knitter, a librarian, a moody teenager. "You know all these people, I suppose."

"Let's see, I know Lillian and Imogene from when I lived here with Agatha."

"Here in this house?"

"Part of my senior year. See, my mother got put away for killing my English teacher and Miss McGee took me in."

"How horrible."

"It was horrible. But Agatha became my substitute mother for six or eight months, so it wasn't all bad. I mean living here sort of straightened me out, you might say." Beverly looked suddenly downcast. "I've never told her how much it meant to me. I came here Saturday to tell her, but I never did."

"Well, she's been pretty busy."

"It isn't that. It's just that I can't tell her without breaking up. I mean she's so old and all. I thought she was old when I lived here and that was years ago. Now she's *really* old and it breaks my heart to think she won't be around forever."

"If you can't do it, I'll tell her for you," Linda offered.

Agatha, in the bedroom, was lecturing Calista, sitting beside her on the bed. "You've got to stand up to him. Think of all the years ahead of you. Think of the future of Willoughby. Now's the time to change the chemistry between you. If you don't, you're going to have a miserable life out there together."

"But what do I say?" Her voice was small and timid. "Dort was always the one to make him settle down. She always knew what to say."

"Then think what she said. You're Dort now, don't forget."

Thinking back, Calista smiled. "One time she told him to buzz off."

"And what else? 'Buzz off' doesn't strike me as very forceful."

"I don't know, she just put her foot down and he got better."

"Then put your foot down. You have to do it before he leaves in the morning." She handed Calista Dort's glasses. "And get rid of that hairnet, for goodness sake."

"Oh, I couldn't do that, I always wear a hairnet."

"Dort never wore hairnets, did she?"

"No, but she was about to start."

"Nonsense, nobody wears a hairnet these days."

"Agatha." Calista faced away from her, hiding her tears. "I don't think I can go through with it. I don't see how I can be Dort."

Agatha rose from the bed. "It's too late for that. Don't you see, if you can't be Dort, you expose me as a liar. Now fix yourself up and come out and join us for hot dogs."

Returning to the kitchen, Agatha found her guests engrossed in Linda Schwartzman's treatise on divorce. ". . . I tell you nobody had a quicker divorce than Manny and I. Actually I was Manny's second wife so he'd had some practice at it, but these days you don't need practice. I mean, thank God for no-fault divorce. Neither party has to prove infidelity or cruel and inhuman treatment or anything. You just file and agree on a settlement and one of you shows up in court and it's over. The sticky part is usually the settlement, but not in our case. I told Manny I didn't want any alimony. My friends told me I was nuts but I've got a profession—why should I spend the rest of my life dependent on a guy I don't even like anymore? I told Manny I needed a computer and a car, so he bought me a new little Honda and gave me a laptop from the mortuary and I was out of there."

Imogene piped up. "Is he still available? I could use a computer and a car."

Agatha noticed that everyone except Lillian and herself laughed at this—even Frederick chuckled a bit and Howie hid a smile—but she and Lillian knew that Imogene wasn't trying to be funny. Imogene didn't make jokes.

Beverly's divorces were more difficult, and even less rewarding. "Terry's dad was a lawyer—Terry Anderson was my first husband—and our divorce dragged on for months until I gave up and just left. Then last fall, when I broke up with B. W. Cooper, he didn't have any more money than I did. So I've come away from two marriages with no alimony, no car, no computer, no nothing."

Imogene's admiring eyes were still fastened on the mortician. "I could really use a car and a computer," she said.

So there have been three divorces among my seven women guests, thought Agatha. Sixty or seventy years ago, in her youth, there hadn't been three divorces in the entire town of Staggerford. John Richard's parents were the only divorced couple she knew in those days. Mr. Richard was living in Rookery, it was said, with a woman not his wife while Mrs. Richard remained in town with John, who was the most miserable creature in Agatha's grade. John would regularly wet his pants in school and be sent home to change. A few incorrigible boys made fun of him. One day at morning recess, when John was once more slouching off on his way home for dry pants, a bunch of them started chanting, "Johnny, Johnny, pee your pants, Johnny, Johnny, pee your pants." Johnny turned and picked up a handful of gravel and tossed it ineffectually at the boys and then hurried away, crying. It was his tears that aroused Agatha to action. Seeing their teacher Sister Mary Charles occupied with girls on the teeter-totter on the far side of the playground, she took it upon herself to stop the chanters. She came up behind their perennial leader, Harry Plotzky, and, grabbing him by the belt, gave him a violent shake while shouting, "Stop it, stop it," in his ear. He was startled into silence and so were his cohorts. Now, recalling the incident, she was amazed that they didn't turn on her, didn't attack her or at least start chanting, "Goody-two-shoes," or some worse insult. All her life she'd exerted this surprising sort of control over people, as though she'd been born with some mysterious and unanswerable kind of authority.

"You two girls are quite the show-offs," said Howie, starting to be a nuisance again. He'd picked up on the word "alimony" and insisted that Linda and Beverly were showing off because the word "settlement" would have done just as well.

Agatha came to their defense. "Actually 'alimony' is the shorter word, Howard. 'Settlement' has the same number of syllables and more letters."

Howie, unimpressed with logic even as a sixth grader, replied, "It ain't the shortness of it or the longness of it. It's the strangeness. It's just a dang strange word and I don't see why people have to say it when a perfectly good ordinary word will do. You'd never catch me saying 'alimony.'"

This grew into a tirade that soon emptied the kitchen of most of the women. They went into the living room, where they exchanged pained looks while listening to Howie continue his spiel, which he couldn't seem to find the end of. They were startled suddenly by a female voice who ended it for him by shouting, "Howie, shut up! Do you understand 'shut up'? Now shut up!" It wasn't until Howie's mumbled objections were met with "Just shut up and buzz off," that Agatha realized the voice belonged to Calista. A moment later a much subdued Howie emerged from the kitchen with Frederick and the two of them retired quietly to the sunroom.

Later, Agatha climbed the stairs to bed and heard Imogene, below her in the living room, explaining to Linda Schwartzman, "Mother and I have never owned a car, you see, and my computer's on the fritz."

She was kept awake by the thought of so many hearts beating

under her roof. Surely not even her gregarious parents had ever en-
tertained nine overnight guests. And what an odd lot they were.
Linda Schwartzman, statuesque, energetic, overly made up, with
large features, her mouth and eyes especially. Beverly Bingham
Cooper with her rough edges, her hawklike look—deep-set eyes
and large nose. She was a very deliberate storyteller—no quick ges-
tures, no quick words. Janet Raft Meers, a hardscrabble girl who
cleaned up and moved easily into Staggerford's society, a cheerful
presence with an empathetic heart. Her daughter, Sara, a cute and
whining teenager with black, snappy eyes, an undeveloped figure
and a telephone attached to her ear. Imogene was the unhappiest
person on earth; her favorite pastime was finding people dumber
than herself and either lecturing or ridiculing them. Her mother,
snoring gently at my side, after a lifetime of being softly passive, has
begun to surprise me and—yes, I admit it—frighten me with her
occasional bark. Then there were the two men. Howard Holister
was simply a neurotic nutcase. Dear Frederick had a large heart and
a small ego—what an agreeable combination when compared to its
opposite; he had a stoop-shouldered, hangdog appearance as
though he were ashamed of being so tall, and his squint, acquired
by sitting outside all summer in the sun had nearly closed his left
eye for good.

Then a moment before sleep the image of her brother, who
died when she was eight, appeared in her imagination, as he so often had done since Frederick moved in with her. Frederick reminded her of Timothy, both men being tall, quiet presences
around the house; both men slept in this room. She loved Timothy
inordinately and, like her parents, was devastated by his death from
influenza at the age of nineteen.

Tonight she pictured him the day his dog died. The dog's name
was Jippie. Her brother didn't often require a confidant, because
during his first eight years as an only child he'd learned the art of

conversing with himself, but on those occasions when he needed to say private things out loud, Jippie was his listener. Jippie was a mixed-blood terrier, white with black spots. He barked at only a few people, not everyone, who walked past the house. He took a particular dislike to a certain Mr. Davenport, who used to mutter insults in the dog's direction on his way downtown. Maybe it was Mr. Davenport who fed him ground glass and brought about his agonizing death under the lilac bush in the backyard the year Timothy was fourteen and Agatha was six. This was her first experience of death and she hated it, but following her brother's stoical example she showed no emotion. She sat on the front step of the house and watched Timothy play catch with himself by throwing a tennis ball against the wall while their father buried the dog in the backyard. It took their father a long time, because the earth was very dry and hard that summer. Timothy didn't stop playing catch until he heard their father put the shovel in the garage and start the car to go downtown to his law office.

"God keep Timothy, God keep all the faithful departed," she murmured to the dark as she turned over and fell asleep.

TUESDAY

Waking again at dawn, Agatha hurried to the window and saw that the flood had drawn back several feet from the cars parked in her backyard. She also saw Frederick digging a hole in the grass near the cars and thought once again of her father burying the dog. She watched until her curiosity was satisfied: Frederick brought out the slop pail from the back porch and buried its contents.

"Lillian," she called, "the water's down below your doorsill, alleluia."

There was no response. Seeing no movement in the blanketed lump on Lillian's side of the bed, she wondered if her friend had died in the night. She went and laid a hand on the blanket. "Do you hear me? The flood is receding."

There was a slight stirring. "I hear you—what time is it?"

"Twenty to six."

Lillian groaned and gave her body a defiant flop. "Too early. I never get up before eight."

"Yesterday you were up at this time."

"You *got* me up."

Dressing, Agatha asked, "What's gotten into you, Lillian? What's eating you? You've never been a resentful person. You've never been touchy. Ever since you were a girl you were always cooperative and friendly. But now you've changed."

Another groan, another flop.

"You've become testy, Lillian, and I want to know . . . if it's something I've done . . . or if you're like this to people generally. I have to say it's not very becoming."

She was answered by silence, so she went downstairs, passed quietly through the living room so as not to wake Imogene, and found Frederick in the kitchen supplying Howie with bread and peanut butter. The radio was on, proclaiming the danger past in places like Rookery, Willoughby, and Staggerford. High water had moved downriver to Detroit Lakes and Gopher Prairie, toward Fargo.

"They're getting ahead of themselves, aren't they?" said Agatha. "The water's still plenty high around here."

"It'll be only a day or two till we're back to normal," Frederick replied.

"But think of the poor souls who've been flooded. It'll be years."

Frederick said, "But it's gone down a foot and a half—that's the main thing."

"Please, Frederick, optimism isn't very becoming to you." Nor did it feel very natural to Frederick. Both he and his Aunt Agatha had grown pessimistic with age, and it was only lately that, in order to counter their gloomy remarks, he'd fallen into the habit of saying optimistic things.

"We gotta go," announced Howie, standing up from the table, peanut butter on his chin.

"What's your hurry?" she asked.

He headed for the back door with a desperate look in his eye. "We gotta get out of here before my sister wakes up." He slipped into his jacket as he hurried around the house to the front porch and climbed into the boat, which was partially grounded. Frederick gulped down his milk and was about to follow when Agatha cautioned him:

"You'll have to wear more clothes. There's a stiff breeze from the north."

He agreed. She followed him to the closet in the front entryway, where she insisted that he put on, besides his scarf and cap, his
olive drab, fur-lined trench coat, which he had recently bought for
four dollars at the Salvation Army store.

"Thank you, Frederick, you've been a lifesaver."

"Any time," he said and hurried off.

Later, after everyone had eaten snack food for breakfast, another
boat tied up at Agatha's house, and a man and a woman stepped up
onto the porch. The man, bewhiskered and shivering in a light
windbreaker, looked to Linda Schwartzman, who went to the door,
like a derelict. "Hi," he said, trying to peer around her into the living room. "Is Miss McGee in?"

Linda laughed. "Of course she is—where would she possibly
go in this flood? Who shall I say is asking?"

"Tell her Lee Fremling." Then, turning to the tall, very thin
young woman at his side, he added, "And Leslie Hokanson, editor
of the *Weekly.*" Ms. Hokanson was obviously partial to black. Her
shoes, her tight slacks, her coat, as well as her eyes and hair, were
black. So was her lipstick.

Linda summoned her hostess: "Agatha, the media wants you."

"So I see," said Agatha from her chair, because the two visitors
had followed Linda into the living room.

"Hi," said the laconic publisher, standing at a distance with his
hands in the pockets of his jacket, his hair mussed either by the wind
or poor grooming. "This is Leslie Hokanson I told you about, Miss
McGee. We were jist wonderin' if we could get an interview."

"About the state of my health, no doubt."

"No, about bein' stranded in the high water." A thought
crossed his mind that suddenly animated his face, caused his eyes to
brighten for a moment. "When Mulholland came into the paper

this morning and mentioned you, Les here came up with the perfect headline. AGATHA'S ARK, she says, just like that, right off the top of her head. Then she asked me, did I suppose you'd give her an interview. I said I figured you would, because there's no way you'd let a headline as good as that go to waste."

Leslie Hokanson raised a camera to her eye, focusing on Agatha, who said, "No pictures of me," as the shutter clicked. When she focused again, Agatha called out, "Don't you understand English?"

Click, click.

"Here," said Sara Meers delightedly, flying over to stand in front of the camera. "You can interview me."

Glad of Sara's presence for once, Agatha said, "You may interview any of my guests who trust you, Miss Hokanson. But not me. Nor will you print any photo of me in your rag. You wrote those falsehoods about my alleged bronchitis and heart condition. Surely my doctor didn't give you that information."

Ignoring her, Editor Hokanson beckoned Sara into a far corner of the room, where she drew a tiny tape recorder from the pocket of her coat, held it up to Sara's mouth, and asked her a question. Publisher Fremling, meanwhile, sank into the couch next to Imogene and explained with a self-satisfied smile: "I talked to Les about that article, Miss McGee. She got the information from a reliable source."

"From whom?"

"Oh, I can't tell you that."

"Can't or won't."

He thought over his options before replying, "Won't. Because it's a confidential source. Can't, because it'd be against the law."

"What law, pray tell?"

"The state supreme court last year upheld the confidentiality of informants."

"Oh bosh." Agatha took a moment to subdue her emotion,

then said evenly, "Surely you can tell me." She, in disgust, turned to look outside, this man being too stupid to reason with.

But then he told her. "It's Rebecca O'Donnell, nurse at the clinic. She's a friend of Les's. Once in a while, if we need a little filler, Les'll call Rebecca and ask what's going on. Usually it's nothing much but once in a while she hits the jackpot."

"I?" said Agatha. "I am the jackpot?"

Fremling nodded. "Yep, good enough for page two. I s'pose when Mayor Druppers gets sick he'll be on the front page, but he's about the only one. Most people are on page eight. By the way, Miss McGee, I guess you knew the old lady who died in Willoughby the other day. Mulholland says you've got her sister stayin' here with you. I'm puttin' together her obituary and I'm lookin' for some filler." Getting no answer from Agatha, he turned to Imogene and said, "Are you her?" then immediately corrected himself. "Oh no, you're in the library."

Agatha turned to see Imogene glowering at him, her cheeks turning an angry red. His correction had obviously done nothing to quell her fury at being mistaken for a Holister sister.

The editor with the tape recorder, having finished with Sara, moved to the dining room table, where Beverly and Janet were playing rummy and giggling at some secret joke while Calista sat absently watching them.

Fremling said, "Miss McGee, I asked you . . ."

"And I heard you," she said. "Rather than trouble her sister in her grief . . . I can answer your questions about Calista Holister." She had decided that this would be the safer method of sustaining her deception.

But then Calista stepped into the room. "Did somebody call my name?"

"No, Dort," said Agatha, crestfallen, fully expecting her to give away their secret. "He was just asking about Calista."

Putting on Dort's glasses, Calista was transformed. She gave Lee Fremling a serene smile and said, "She was my sister, you know. I am the Willoughby postmistress." She went on telling him about her dead sister's upright character and health problems as Agatha listened tensely, expecting the worst. But Calista did a marvelous job of it, without a hitch, without once calling her sister Dort.

These visitors didn't stay long. They were gone in time for the household to gather in the kitchen for *Lolly Speaking* on the radio. The wheezy voice of Lolly Edwards began with a recipe for asparagus soup, and then spent six or eight minutes on a firsthand description of "just the most magnificent wedding reception" held at Anderson's Resort on Bloodsucker Lake. Finally, with about five minutes left, she turned to the flood, speaking by phone to a man in Rookery who said the water had gone down considerably since Sunday and nearly all the streets were drivable except in the Lancy Park neighborhood, where gawkers had been interfering with people returning to assess the damage to their homes. Next she called the Jiffystop Station in Willoughby, and Inga told her that the lower end of town was still partially under water, but it was going down fast. She expected all highways in the area to be open tomorrow and businesses to be functioning as usual.

"Businesses? What businesses? I thought yours was the only business in Willoughby."

"Oh my, no," replied Inga, "we've got Samantha's Donut Shop and Benji's Bar, and we've still got our post office, you know."

"And now," said Lolly—and then interrupting herself with a lengthy siege of coughing—"what you've all been waiting for. Agatha McGee! The dear soul, she hasn't been at all well, housebound and suffering from heart trouble and I don't know what all. Leland and I visited her last week in Staggerford, and I've been worried sick ever since, because her lovely house is on the street next to the Badbattle River where it flows through town. What are you shaking your head for, Rod? My producer, Rod Browning, is shaking his head." There was another coughing spell of some duration, before she asked, "What's that, Rod? No connection! What do you mean no connection? Well, call the phone company. You did? What did they say?"

There was the sound of shuffling papers and a series of loud reports, as if somebody was bumping the microphone, then: "All right, listeners, we're going to change tack here this morning. It seems phone service is out in Staggerford, so we're going to talk more about flood relief, and to do that we're going to go to Congressman Dale Lindquist. Have you got him on the wire, Rod? Okeydokey, here we go. Hello, Congressman, and how's the weather in Washington this morning?"

It took a minute to get through the preliminaries before Lolly asked about the prospect of financial help for flood victims.

"Low interest loans, that will be Berrington County's windfall if she's declared a disaster area. I'm lobbying the president this morning to have all of central Minnesota declared a disaster area. How's the airport in Rookery, Lolly? I'm flying home tomorrow to have a look around, and also to attend a funeral in Willoughby."

Agatha and Calista exchanged an apprehensive look.

"The airport's closed—it's pretty soggy. You'd better land in Fargo or Duluth." Cough, cough. "Is it the Holister woman's funeral? I didn't know you knew the Holisters."

"Oh they're old friends of mine. I met them when I first ran for office. They're dyed-in-the-wool Democrats, great contributors to the party—not that they won't have a bipartisan funeral of course. I don't mean our friendship is political in any way. No, I'm just saying how we happened to meet years ago. Oh yes, we're old, old friends."

Calista shook her head and began to object, but she was shushed by Agatha.

"I talked to the Holister brother Henry just this morning. It seems he'd been out in a boat delivering food to flood victims—saved the lives of a whole houseful of starving women in Stagger-ford, he says—and now he's back in the post office seeing that the mail goes through. What a guy, eh, Lolly? Anyhow Henry says the funeral will be the day after tomorrow. He says the church in Willoughby's on high ground and the cemetery's on high ground, so there's no reason to wait any longer."

"I don't have a brother named Henry, do I?" said Calista, look-ing bewildered and worried, as if she'd forgotten some essential part of Agatha's ruse.

"Of course not. The congressman's always getting people's names wrong. At Father Finn's farewell party last fall, he kept call-ing him Father Fogarty."

"Did I hear that right?" said Linda Schwartzman. "Did he say when the funeral is?"

"Day after tomorrow," said Janet.

"Since when? What right does a congressman in Washington have to schedule a funeral in Minnesota?"

Calista spoke up. "My brother's to blame for that. He's so mouthy, he'll say anything that comes into his head—true or not true, it's all the same to him. Don't pay any attention."

When Lolly Edwards went off the air, Beverly followed Janet upstairs, where they stayed for half an hour or more, and then Janet came down alone.

"What are you two hatching up there?" Agatha wanted to know.

"Beverly's trying on some of my clothes. She's got a date tonight. My jeans don't fit her, but my blouses do."

"Are you both out of your minds? How can she go out on a date?"

"She called William Mulholland Sunday night before the phone went dead and he asked her to have supper with him tonight. He's coming to pick her up in a boat."

Lillian, passing through the room, heard this and her eyes lit up. She went directly to the stairs and started up.

"Lillian," called Agatha, "it's none of our business."

Lillian paused briefly on the third step and turned to Agatha with a wordless smile, her first smile in weeks, a smile of such pure pleasure that Agatha wondered if her friend's dark mood was connected somehow with the lack of gossip in this house. Lillian in her old age had become addicted to NEWS OF THE HEART, as one of her favorite tabloids called it in a sweeping banner across the front page each week. And what had become of those dreadful tabloids, Agatha wondered. Until some weeks ago, Lillian always carried two or three of them, along with her mail, in her knitting bag, and took surreptitious peeks at them when she thought Agatha wasn't watching.

"Hey, look at the water," called Sara, pointing out the front window.

Agatha and Janet went over and saw the water receding before their eyes. The top of the retaining wall at the front edge of Agatha's yard was soon exposed. Standing with one arm across Sara's shoulders and the other around Janet's waist, she watched the level go gradually down on the useless wall of sandbags at the river's edge. Linda came in from the kitchen and joined them, then Imogene, then Calista. The six of them stood there for a long time, sighing now and then, unable to take their eyes off the spectacle, unable to find words to express their relief.

Later, with the water down to street level, Linda and Imogene went out into the windy afternoon to check on their respective houses. Linda was first to return. She reported that her foundation held, but because of the water in her basement, there was an intolerable dampness throughout the house. Imogene found her house in worse shape—silt covering the floors and the lower part of the walls. "Damn it, damn it," she cried, shaking her fist at the ceiling. "Our rugs are history and so are the couch and the over-stuffed chair in the living room. In the kitchen everything in the lower cupboards is soaked. And the smell!—the whole house is full of the most awful smell."

Unaccountably her mother seemed cheered by this awful news. The contentious scowl she'd been wearing for weeks was lifted from her face.

The phone rang and Agatha was saying hello before her guests realized what a life-saving phenomenon the restoration of phone service was, and they broke out in a cheer. It was William Mulholland calling to say that he was on his way to pick up Beverly for dinner.

Then Janet called home and learned from Stephen that the house had been spared from damage, but the road and yard were a muddy mess. He'd have to wait for the road to dry out before he could come to town.

"What have you been doing with yourself all this time alone?" Janet asked.

"Watching videos. Hey, Ma, I didn't know you had *Kiss of Death*. Our film professor showed us *Kiss of Death*, the old one, not the new one. It's got Richard Widmark in it."

"Is your father home?"

"He just called from Rookery, said he thought he'd be able to come home tomorrow. Richard Widmark's so cool. He plays this psychotic killer. He ties up an old lady and pushes her down a long flight of stairs in her wheelchair."

Then it was Beverly's turn to call Berrington. She talked for only a moment to her son's supervisor at the halfway house, but this was enough to set her off once again, after she hung up, on her obsession. "Poor Owen doesn't have much going for him." She was addressing Agatha and the others in the living room. "He's a weak-willed alcoholic with no training in any worthwhile field, and he's schizophrenic besides. Say this program in Berrington lets him recover to where he was before he started drinking—what then? No skills to build on, no ambition except to own a car. He started drinking in the ninth grade. Booze makes him absolutely bonkers. We lived at Fort Chafee when he was a ninth grader. This was before his mental illness showed up. He had this friend named Sam who he used to stay overnight with sometimes, and what Terry and I didn't know was that Sam's parents would be gone and Sam and Owen would drink all night. Of course we knew something was wrong—I mean he'd come home and sleep all the next day—but we were so stupid it took us months to catch on. Well, when Terry finally figured it out, *he* went absolutely ballistic. He acted like a drill sergeant, screaming at Owen at the top of his voice. The first time he hit him, I said that's it. I walked out. I left Terry and took Owen with me. You've got to stop me if I go on about this stuff too long. I mean neurosis, psychosis, addiction, shock treatment, tranquilizers, group therapy, depression, thoughts of suicide, the whole ball of wax. Oh, good, here comes Mr. Mulholland. I'll see you all later."

Later, about to retire early, Agatha confided to Janet that Beverly, having already had two bad husbands, ought not to be going out on dates. "The poor child's a victim," she said, standing at the bottom of the stairway. "She's only looking for more trouble."

Janet disagreed. "Sure, Beverly's made some bad choices, but that doesn't mean she ought to give up on life."

"I'm not saying on life. On *men*."

"But a woman isn't complete without a man in her life." Immediately aware of her faux pas, Janet quickly added, "Some women, I mean."

Agatha smiled mysteriously, bowed her head, and turned to

climb the stairs. Janet went up with her, supporting her by the el-
bow. She went on about Beverly's wisdom and courage, insisting
that when you fell off a horse it was best to get right back on and
ride; otherwise, fear took over. Agatha allowed herself to be lec-
tured all the way to the door of her room, because if Janet had
given her an opening she'd surely have pointed out the poor choice
that Janet herself made, marrying Randy Meers.

Of course the feeling was mutual. Randy Meers, drinking beer in
the bar of the Red Roof Motel, was telling a stranger, a traveling
salesman from Mankato, about what he called his wife's obsession
with Miss McGee. "She drives into town practically every day to
see her, and she comes home full of ideas the old bag plants in her
mind. Like who to see at school about my daughter's poor grade in
civics, and what to do about ants that get into the house in the
summertime and what a lousy husband I am, and she blows up if I
ever say anything negative about this intolerant old bag. And she's
with her right now as I speak. I talked to my son home from college on the phone and he says his mom's been staying at the old
bag's since Saturday. She must have gone to see her as soon as I left
home on Saturday, and she's been stuck there ever since because of
the flood. So what is that?—four days she's been feeding my wife
bad vibes about me. I know just what she's saying. She's saying what
a neglectful husband I am because I'm not home during this flood.
What the hell am I supposed to do, swim? It's like one winter I was
in Loomis showing a house and this blizzard came up and I had to
stay overnight, and the old bag said that was another example of
how I'm never around in a pinch. Same thing the day my daughter
was born, I was here in Rookery for a meeting with my dad's sales
force and I got called out of the meeting by my mom on the phone
saying I had this brand new daughter, and I didn't know a damn

thing about it. I mean how was I supposed to predict it was time, when the kid came two weeks early?"

"Let's go look for some action," said the stranger, slipping on his raincoat. "I hear there's good-looking babes hanging out in the restaurant next door."

"Naw, you go ahead. That's about the only thing the old bag can't accuse me of—adultery—and I'm making sure to keep it that way."

Left alone, he began to repeat his complaint to the bartender, but was interrupted by a couple coming into the bar and needing service. So he gave up and went to his room, where he got into bed with a thick new paperback by Mario Puzo and after a page and a half he fell asleep.

WEDNESDAY

The water level kept falling through the night, so that by morning Janet and Sara were able to drive off down the squishy, rutted alley, delivering Linda Schwartzman downtown to the funeral home and Lillian back to the Sunset Senior Center, and then continuing on home. Beverly drove away a short time later, and Imogene walked to the public library. Forgetting momentarily that Calista was still in her bedroom, Agatha sat down in her customary chair by the window and luxuriated in the sudden solitude and silence. How terrible her yard looked, debris and mud covering her lawn. And how quickly her houseguests fled, she thought, like animals sprung from a zoo. Of course most of them were profuse in their thanks and all promised to return soon—in fact, Linda Schwartzman would be back to spend more nights here until her basement was dry—but Agatha was glad that no one lingered. She was relieved beyond words to have them gone. It wasn't natural to have seven guests for four whole days and nights, at least not natural for Agatha, who grew up more or less as an only child and spent her entire adult life living alone—except for the changing presence in the room she'd often rented out upstairs until Frederick came to occupy it.

River Street was dry, but no traffic moved on it until mid-morning, when the barriers were removed and Father Healy drove up in his little red car. When Agatha saw him stop before climbing the steps to her yard, she realized that he was inspecting her retaining wall. He wore a red sweatshirt and tan slacks.

"You aren't dressed as a clergyman," was the first thing she said to him when he was settled in his chair by the window.

"Some days I don't feel like a clergyman," he replied.

Her frown of reproval deepened. "What's that supposed to mean?"

"I've been so useless in the flood. I haven't helped one person. I had no idea you were trapped here, Miss McGee . . ."

"We came through it just fine, all eight of us."

"It was only this morning I heard."

"There's nothing you could have done."

"I could have at least called you up, given you encouragement over the phone."

"What phone? We were disconnected until last night."

"Oh, my." He shook his head pityingly.

"But as long as we're confessing our sins, Father, let me tell you what I've done. I've told an enormous lie. I've told a lie so powerful that seven or eight other people have been swept along in its wake. Forced to lie as well, you see." It was impossible to hold the story back. She had to tell it in full, compounding her sin by involving a priest of God in her deception. "The way it happened, when my old friend at the Willoughby post office died the other day—"

The priest interrupted her by raising his right hand in blessing and saying, "No need to go into it, Miss McGee. I can give you absolution on the spot."

"Stop it. I can't be forgiven, and it's not forgiveness I'm asking for. To be forgiven I'd have to be contrite and promise never to commit the same sin again, am I not right?"

"That's the old formula all right, out of the catechism."

"Well, I'm contrite, but I'm not making any promises like that. In other words, I don't intend to rectify things. I intend to carry this lie to my grave. And what do you mean the *old* formula? If it's been replaced by a *new* formula, I certainly haven't been told. Anyhow, the other day . . ."

Calista Holister, roused by the priest's entrance, came out of Agatha's bedroom, putting an end to Agatha's confession. Wearing her sister's glasses with the frosted lens, she stepped boldly up to Frank Healy and shook his hand. She said, "I'm Dort Holister, Father, the dead woman's sister."

"Ah, yes. Haven't I seen you at mass in Willoughby?"

"That's right, me and my sister. My brother doesn't go to church."

The priest offered her his place, which she took, and he pulled up a straight chair close beside her and asked how she was bearing up.

"Better than I expected," was her answer, and she went on to describe her sister's last days and death, mixing her own spells of arthritic pain into the story with her sister's hypertension. Glancing at Agatha with a twinkle in her eye, she said, "Poor Calista, there was even a hint of dementia toward the end."

Agatha was both amazed and appalled to witness Calista's taking over her sister's role so completely, at her falsehoods, at her assurance. She was even sitting straight in her chair the way Dort used to.

Walking to work, Imogene planned to convert a part of the book storage room at the rear of the library into her temporary bedroom. Anyplace was better than Agatha's, with all those oddballs crawling about—her own spooky old mother knitting her life away like some automatic textile machine, and that uneducated Bingham woman with her son goofy as a loon, and the big new woman undertaker whose hands had been in contact with God knew what before she shook hands with you, and the old Holister woman, the clinging-vine type if ever there was one. And worst of all—because she occupied a place next to Agatha's heart, where Imogene wanted to be—there was Janet Meers, with her ostentatious house on the river and her empty-headed daughter, Sara. The daughter, having caught a cold while wasting her time fiddling around with sandbags, spent yesterday sneezing all over everybody. It was one of the wonders of the universe how Janet Raft, growing up on a hardscrabble farm with a dead mother and a no-account father living off the county welfare rolls, and then marrying someone as stupid as Randy Meers, had turned into Agatha's favorite.

Unlocking the library, Imogene went directly to the book storage room. She'd forgotten that it was windowless and thus unsuitable as a bedroom. You couldn't be expected—in fact, it was probably illegal—to sleep in a room with no emergency egress in case of fire. Agatha's rooms at least had windows. A few more nights there wouldn't be intolerable, if she got the room upstairs next to Frederick's. This morning, as soon as her assistant arrived at work, Imogene would go down the street to Beaman Realtors and arrange to buy one of the new condos in the Marketplace.

Her mother, meanwhile, arrived at the Sunset Senior Center to find it empty of residents, and a team of workmen noisily vacuuming water out of the hallway carpet on the ground floor. This seemed a good enough reason—despite her apartment being upstairs and high and dry—for her to return to Agatha's for at least one more night.

Janet and Sara Meers, too, were stymied. A washout on the road to their house on the river forced them to head back to the Thrifty Springs Motel.

Beverly Bingham reached her destination, the Hewitt Halfway House on Hewitt Street in Berrington, and found that her son had run away. She, too, returned to Staggerford, and to the city clerk's office, where William Mulholland invited her to accompany him on an inspection tour of the town.

When Calista finished her account of her sister's death, Father Healy turned to Agatha and said, "Miss McGee, isn't it time for *Lolly Speaking?*"

"Goodness, don't tell me you listen to that nonsense."

"Not ordinarily, but you're going to be on today. KRKU's been announcing it all morning."

"I am? Why doesn't Lolly tell me beforehand?" muttered Agatha as she crossed the room to her Magnavox console, a massive, coffinlike piece of furniture purchased by her father in the late fifties, not long before he died. It took her a minute to dial up KRKU, and she caught Lolly Edwards in midsentence, extolling the virtues of the personnel at Shogren's Chevrolet-Buick. For Calista's sake, who was slightly hard of hearing, she turned up the volume, and Lolly's voice came in deep and rich; her phlegmy, bronchial cough sounded as if she were in the room.

The phone rang. Father Healy answered and handed it to Agatha, who turned down the volume. It was Lolly's producer in Rookery, alerting her for the show. Almost immediately Lolly was gushing on the line. "Oh, Miss McGee, you poor dear, we're on the air. To think you've been trapped for the last three days with dozens of people in your lovely house on that lovely street next to the river. My heart goes out to you because I know what a burden overnight company can be for me, and I'm a people person, so for you, Miss McGee, it must have been the pits."

"The pits? Well, yes and no. Actually there were only seven . . ."

"You deserve recognition for this, Miss McGee, and what I'm going to do is tell Mrs. Bush about how you saved the lives of all those people. Surely our First Lady ought to be able to get you a medal of some kind, or, failing that, at least nationwide recognition." Here Lolly's voice diminished and was replaced by a loud coughing spell.

"Never mind Mrs. Bush," said Agatha. "What I want to talk about is your habit of calling people unannounced on the radio. It's a serious imposition and downright impolite."

This was one of those days when Lolly Edwards, coughing or not, forged ahead without listening to her guests.

"And speaking of recognition, Miss McGee, I have to ask if you've scheduled your memorial service yet. If you hold it during a midweek morning, we can air it live. Otherwise, we'll transcribe it for later broadcast. Live or transcribed, of course we'll see to it that you get an audiotape of the proceedings. My one regret about my own memorial service is that nobody recorded it."

"I have to hang up now, good-bye." Agatha couldn't be sure if she'd been heard over the latest fit of coughing, but she cut the connection anyhow. Returning to her two guests, she said, "Lolly Edwards is obsessed with publicity. She can't seem to get enough for herself, and now she's started on me. That's the last time I'm appearing on her show."

Father Healy looked amused while Calista was clealy overawed. "Oh, Agatha," she said, "but that was the actual Lolly Edwards in person. How could you possibly turn her down?"

"It's not hard to turn down a snoop."

"I believe you both know Ms. Schwartzman, the undertaker," said Father Healy. "I've been in touch with her this morning about the funeral. It will have to be either tomorrow or Monday if you want a mass. Day after tomorrow is Good Friday, you see, and I can't say a mass between then and midnight mass on Holy Saturday—tradition has it that way. Of course we could have a funeral service without the mass either day; it's up to you."

"No, it's up to my sister," said Calista. "She always said she wanted to go out with a mass. She had some favorite hymns she wanted sung. 'Ave Maria' and 'Dona Nobis Pacem' were two I remember."

"Then I suggest Monday," said Agatha, hoping that Congressman Lindquist would have to fly back to Washington before he got a look at the body.

"Oh no!" said Calista adamantly. "Calista's been dead since Saturday. That would be over a week."

Agatha acceded. At least tomorrow fewer people would know about the funeral, friends who knew Dort well enough not to be fooled.

"Tomorrow it is then," said the priest. "We'll hold it at three o'clock and I'll notify the *Weekly*. That way it won't go unannounced. How's that?"

"That will be just fine," said Calista, looking greatly relieved, wiping away the last of her tears.

Agatha was eager for more solitude, but Father Healy appeared in no hurry to leave, and she'd have Calista on her hands until Frederick returned with the car. She phoned Willoughby and got Howie on the line. He told her that Frederick was out on his route, and not expected back until three. Howie asked, "How're all you guys doing in that house of yours?"

"Guys? Did we look like guys to you?" She hung up.

"I'll take Ms. Holister home," Father Healy volunteered. "Are you up to coming along, Miss McGee? Surely you'll want a bit of fresh air after your ordeal."

On the road to Willoughby, Agatha turned to Calista in the back seat. "Remember, Dort, unless you put your foot down, Howard will soon be out of control. And remember, too, that the survival of the post office is up to you. And therefore the future of the town lies in your hands." It was for Calista's sake alone that Agatha had agreed to ride along. She had anticipated a long midday snooze, but was afraid Calista would soon weaken and spill the beans to the priest.

She needn't have worried. "I haven't told you, Agatha . . ." Calista strained to raise her thin voice over the sound of the car. "I'm getting new glasses. I've started catching glimpses of things out of my right eye, and the doctor says I could eventually see as good as new out of it." She covered her mouth to hide a small, secret laugh. "Isn't that good news, Agatha?"

"Indeed, it's miraculous. Especially since you lost your eye to cancer."

If Father Healy were listening to this exchange, he showed no sign of it.

They saw devastation wherever they looked. Water standing in fields. Low-lying farmsteads standing in deep pools. Drowned cattle lying in pastures. Where the highway had been covered with water the other day, there was now no highway at all. WASHOUT said the sign directing them on a detour.

As Frederick and Howie predicted, Willoughby's main street had been spared, its few public enterprises and St. James's Church and cemetery hadn't been touched. Father Healy, carrying Calista's bag, followed his two passengers through the street door and into the business end of the post office. There was a wall of mailboxes with glass doors and combination dials. They found Billy and Inga Wentworth, from the Jiffystop Station across the road, visiting with Howie through his grill. Agatha introduced Father Healy to all three of them.

"The brother of the deceased, I assume," said the priest, shaking Howie's sweaty hand.

"Dang it to heck!" said Howie, addressing his friends. "There's another one of them hundred-dollar words. Dort ain't deceased, she's dead!"

Agatha nudged his sister into action. "Listen here!" Calista said forcefully, adjusting Dort's glasses on her nose as she stepped up to the grill. "That's the last time I want to hear a complaint from you about big words or anything else. And it wasn't Dort who died, it was Calista. Do you understand?"

His demeanor changed immediately. He hung his head like a chastised little boy, but still he took exception. "This guy said deceased," he whined.

"And if you went to church like you should, you'd know this is Father Healy, our parish priest."

There was a moment of silence while the Wentworths marveled at Calista's newfound assertiveness. Then Billy told Agatha he had heard her on the radio that morning. "You ought to be on more often," he said. "You've got a better broadcasting voice than Lolly Edwards. It's hard to listen to her cough all the time."

His wife Inga asked, "When is your memorial service, Agatha? Billy and I want to be there for it."

"There will be no such service. That's Lolly's pipe dream entirely."

"Well, congratulations anyway on your Mrs. Bush medal," said Billy.

"Yes, that's spectacular," said his wife.

This being too ridiculous to deserve a response, Agatha directed Calista, as well as Father Healy with her bag, through the door into the living quarters. She and the priest then bid everyone good-bye and returned to the car.

On the way home, Agatha spilled out her story. She put it in historical perspective by beginning with the founding of Willoughby in 1889. "It sprang up as a marketplace for farmers who had followed the railroad into central Minnesota," she told the priest. "By the turn of the century there were forty-some houses in Willoughby. Twice as many as now. There were two general stores, two saloons, and a pen beside the railroad tracks for shipping cattle. There wasn't any post office. There were two churches, Catholic and English Lutheran. In those days a villager—I forget his name—rode a horse to Staggerford two or three times a week and brought home the mail. It was a round-trip of over fifteen miles, and sometimes if there were big packages . . . he'd have to go back with a buckboard. So Washington was under constant pressure to establish a post office in Willoughby. Well, it made sense. The mail he picked up in Staggerford had already . . . passed through Willoughby on the train. And it happened. Eighty years ago, the year I was born, they opened the Willoughby post office."

Father Healy glanced at Agatha to see if she looked eighty today. No, he determined. She was much more animated and her color was much better than even a week ago. Her voice seemed stronger.

"In all this time, Willoughby has had only four postmasters. John Mahoney served for eight years, until he died of a heart attack while shucking grain. His son Roger Mahoney succeeded him and served thirty-seven years. It was during Roger Mahoney's time that the apartment was built on the back. Upon his death, Herbert Holister was appointed to the job. The Holisters were big Democrats. He'd been a delegate to at least one national convention. Herbert was postmaster for almost thirty years and was followed by his niece Dorothy Holister, otherwise known as Dort. But now, between you and me, Father, Dort is dead. But the world thinks it was Calista."

"Oh, why is that?"

"Because I said so. I told everyone that Calista died, so that the postmaster general . . . wouldn't shut down the Willoughby post office. Which he would have done if Dort were dead. Our congressman, Mr. Lindquist, as well as Mr. Kleinschmidt before him . . . let it be known years ago. 'It remains in operation only until Dort is gone,' they said. They thought it would only be a year or two. Dort had a small stroke fifteen years ago. But she lived on and on. And now she continues to live on and on despite being dead."

"A real survivor."

She gave the priest a scolding look. "This is no time for levity, Father."

"I'm sorry."

"I'm telling you this because I can't hold it back any longer. And because it occurs to me that you might call her by the wrong name at the graveside tomorrow. You know, 'We commit our sister Calista to the earth, Oh Lord,' and so on. That would be the wrong name." Agatha suddenly lost control of herself. "Oh, Lord, now you and I are both in so deep—" Tears sprang into her eyes. She tried to speak, but feeling Father Healy's comforting hand on her shoulder, she was silenced by shame and weeping.

"But your motives were good ones," he told her. "Saving the post office, saving your nephew's job."

Through her tears, she said, "Father, don't accuse me of a motive that selfish. Saving the post office saves much more than Frederick's job. It saves the entire town of Willoughby." She explained, then, about its long decline, the loss of the railroad, the loss of its public school, and its certain decimation if it lost the mail.

"Well, then, you're in the clear as far as your lie is concerned."

She looked skeptical, unconvinced.

"You acted out of altruistic purpose."

"A lie is a lie, Father."

"Sometimes a lie is a white lie, not serious, a little fib."

She considered this and wanted to believe it, but couldn't. "I shouldn't have to remind you, Father, that every lie is a mortal sin."

"It is?"

"Of course. Because it chips away at the moral fabric of the human race. I was taught that as a girl."

He turned to her and said, "I was reading a novel last night and came across a statement to the effect that morality is not necessarily something to base human behavior on."

"Who would write such an irresponsible thing? Hemingway, I suppose."

"A British woman named Penelope Fitzgerald."

"The English aren't to be trusted."

They pulled into town and were distracted by the sight of houses along Hemlock Avenue that had been almost totally submerged. They were all the color of mud. Patio furniture lay sprawled on the roof of one. On another lay a garbage can and a bicycle.

"Oh my, how dreadful."

"Yes, it's terrible, and I had no idea it was this bad."

Approaching her house, Agatha saw more serious damage than she imagined. Part of her retaining wall, eaten away by water, had spilled soil across the front sidewalk and out into the boulevard. Her discouragement at the sight of this mess became bound up with her guilt and caused a pain in her breast, an ache strong enough to make her wish she had company again, to help keep her mind on other things.

"There's your friend Mrs. Kite," said Father Healy, pointing ahead to the figure sitting on Agatha's porch steps, reading a newspaper.

"Lillian," exclaimed Agatha. "What's she doing here?"

Lillian, recognizing the car, came down to street level to ask the priest if he'd been to the public library and met Imogene yet.

"No, I'm sorry," he said, coming around to help Agatha up from her low seat. He promised to do so soon.

"It's just as well you haven't," Lillian told him. "She's not being nice these days."

Agatha saw that her newspaper was *The National Enquirer*, with a picture of Jacqueline Onassis on the front.

The priest was about to help Agatha up the steps but Lillian waved him away. "It's okay, Father, I've got her." The two of them climbed to the front yard and turned and watched him drive away.

"You're back so soon," said Agatha.

"The busloads they took to Berrington aren't back yet, so the senior center's empty. You know I can't stand to be in a building with nobody else in it. Besides, I figured you'd want some help washing bedsheets."

"I do. Thank you, Lillian."

"I was so surprised to find your door locked. Where've you been?"

"To Willoughby, taking Calista home. I mean Dort."

"No, you mean Calista. You can't fool me, Agatha. I've known the Holisters as long as you have. What's going on?"

"Come in, and I'll tell you all about it."

"Your eyes look funny, Agatha, like you've been crying."

"It's being outside without my dark glasses."

As they prepared lunch in the kitchen—a can of tomato soup doctored up with basil and rosemary—Agatha elicited a promise of secrecy from Lillian, and then told her about her plan to save Willoughby. Lillian was astonished. She had thought Agatha's problem with the Holister sisters was mental confusion, not a scheme to defraud the federal government. "You could be in for some real trouble," she told her.

"I know," said Agatha. "But do you suppose I'll be condemned to hell for one sin? I'm counting on God's being more merciful than that."

"I don't mean hell, I mean federal prison. Here, I'll show you." She found a page of her tabloid displaying two photos of a certain Harold Campbell of Campwood, Arkansas. In one he was smiling and nicely dressed in a suit and tie, in the other he had a jacket over his head and was being stuffed into a squad car. "He didn't pay his taxes," Lillian explained. "Five years in the slammer."

Agatha looked bewildered. "I've never been delinquent in paying my taxes."

"Defrauding Uncle Sam will get you at least five years."

Agatha stared at the page.

"Five years is the minimum sentence," Lillian added. "Paroled in three for good behavior."

"Who got five years?" asked Imogene, striding into the kitchen, feeling proud of herself for having finally bought a condo in the Marketplace and full of fear over the loan she agreed to. "Who're you talking about?"

Agatha thrust the paper into her hands and tended to her tea.

The three of them lunched at the table, Imogene uninvited and carrying on about the outrageous price of property. Her mother was still absorbed in her paper.

"Did you know the aliens from Roswell, New Mexico, are being kept in Dayton, Ohio?"

"Can either of you guess what they're charging for interest on a house loan these days? Eight and a quarter percent. *Eight and a quarter percent!*"

"Says right here, the Wright Patterson Air Base, Hangar Nine."

"Why, I'm going to be paying on that place for thirty years, and it's going to be ten years before I make even a small dent in the principle."

In wishing for companionship, this wasn't what Agatha had in mind.

"Wouldn't you just love to have a peek at those creatures? They say they've got real big eyes and they haven't got any hair."

"In thirty years I'll be a decrepit old lady. Why, I'll be eighty. God!"

You'll be old and you may be decrepit, thought Agatha, but you'll never be a lady.

After lunch Imogene announced that she'd need a bedroom for at least three more nights before she could move into her condo, and then she hiked off to work. Agatha, to prevent Lillian from reading to her, went to her own bedroom and lay down for a nap.

Lillian gently nudged her out of a nightmare to say good-bye. Frederick was about to give her a ride back to the senior center. "The sheets are all washed and dried and put back on the beds except this one," she said.

"Sheets?" said Agatha, temporarily disoriented. In her dream she and her grandfather were lost at sea.

"And I left my newspaper on your kitchen table so you and Frederick can read about the aliens. Frederick says he's interested."

"What time is it?"

"It's about three-thirty. I'll see you tomorrow at the funeral."

Agatha, left alone in the still house, lay there for a few minutes, gathering up the details of her conscious life. So Frederick was home, thank the Lord. Once Linda Schwartzman and Imogene leave we'll be back to normal around here. Lillian, too, seems back to normal. Her old agreeable self. Not so testy. What in the world was eating her? Tomorrow after the funeral she will ask her. Oh, the funeral. If Congressman Lindquist is there, he'll recognize Dort and the lie will surely be found out.

Please spare me, O Lord, from prison, hell, and the briny deep.

THURSDAY

Wearing his freshly starched white shirt from the cleaners—Agatha, her stamina waning, had stopped ironing his shirts—and his dark blue necktie with the food stains mostly invisible, Frederick slipped into his six-dollar tweed sport coat from Goodwill and went downstairs to present himself for inspection.

"Yes, Frederick, you look very nice," said Agatha, reaching up and tugging his necktie into a straight line. He expected this approval, since her eyesight was bad. He had resigned himself to the fact that if she had cataract surgery, which Lillian had been pressing her to do, he'd have to buy a new tie.

She herself was wearing her gray suit of a rich nubby material, with a black scarf at her throat. After spending the morning at Nora's Beauty Nook, she had a new permanent that displeased her and she kept putting her hand to her hair, patting it down here and there. On her feet, because she expected to have to walk across the uneven ground of the cemetery, she had decided to wear her high-top, lace-up shoes instead of something more stylish. Stuffing her rosary and a wad of Kleenex into her purse, she asked, "Will we be taking our coats, Frederick?"

It was a lovely warm afternoon, but he'd learned not to make decisions for her, so he went to the front closet and awaited her judgment. "Yes, we'll take them," she said. "A cemetery is always chilly."

They picked up Lillian at Sunset Senior, and, giving themselves plenty of time because of the detour, they arrived at St. James's in Willoughby at the same time as the corpse. The three of them fell into step behind Linda Schwartzman, who helped her young assistant push the coffin on silent wheels into the church and park it in the vestibule.

"Dort tells me that her sister wanted a closed coffin," said Ms. Schwartzman as she unlatched it and lifted the lid. "So we'll close it again after the family has a chance to view the body."

How fiendishly clever Calista had suddenly become, thought Agatha with relief as she stepped up to the coffin. A closed coffin cut the risk of discovery in half. Now if Calista could successfully play her sister's role all afternoon, they'd be in the clear.

At first sight of the body, Agatha was dismayed to see that it didn't resemble the Dort she knew for sixty years. Nor would anyone mistake her for Calista. "The mouth is wrong," said Lillian. It was true. It was no doubt unavoidable since the undertaker never saw Dort alive, but her mouth, a straight line, was all wrong. As far back as she could remember, all Holisters, including Howie, had little bow-shaped lips. And her gray hair—done up by Nora, she was told this morning in the Beauty Nook—looked too finished. Dort was never careful about her hair.

Billy and Inga Wentworth accompanied Calista down the street and into the vestibule. Calista seemed unsteady on her feet as she crossed to the coffin. The three of them stood there for a minute and then, at the sound of car doors closing, turned away. "Are you all right?" Agatha asked her.

"Oh, I'm fine, Agatha. It's just this frosted lens makes it hard to walk, but I thought I'd better wear it to the funeral at least."

"Where's Howard?"

"Outside. He'll come in when they shut the casket. Howie can't stand death, you know."

"So he's the reason it's going to be closed?"

"Oh, yes, he's horribly afraid of seeing a dead person."

This elicited from Agatha a statement she never thought she'd utter: "Thank God for Howard."

At the approach of voices, Agatha realized that Linda Schwartzman was no longer in the vestibule. "Frederick!" she said in a panic. "Close the coffin, quick!"

Turning from the open doorway, where he'd been gazing out at the lovely afternoon, he obediently strode toward the body, but then he hesitated as a number of chattering people came through the door. So Lillian hurried over to the coffin, lowered the lid, and clicked it shut.

"I knew I'd see you today, Miss McGee, and sure enough here you are." This gushy voice, and the cough that accompanied it, belonged to none other than Lolly Edwards. She had two men and a woman with her. One of the men was her son Leland; the other she introduced as Ron, her radio engineer. The woman, a small, pretty, anorexic-looking brunette, was her daughter-in-law, Mary Sue.

"I'm just along for the ride," said Mary Sue with a sidelong glance at Lolly and an ironic twist to her lips, as if she meant more than she'd said.

After stepping up and gathering Agatha into her arms, engulfing her in an overpowering scent of lilac, Lolly instructed the engineer to hurry and get his equipment ready to tape an interview.

"Do you cover all funerals?" Agatha inquired.

To her great relief, Lolly responded, "Oh my, no, I'm here to interview our congressman. Did you know he's coming today?"

"So I've heard. But you just interviewed him the other day on your show."

"Oh, that doesn't count, that was only a phone interview. I find a live interview is much more alive, if you know what I mean."

"But it won't be live when your audience hears it. It will be recorded."

"Well, if you're going to be picky, I probably should have said 'face-to-face.'" She said this with no sign of resentment in her smiley expression, and then added pleasantly, "Are you always such a difficult piece of work, Miss McGee, or am I catching you at a bad time?"

They were interrupted by a shriek of grief from the doorway as Nora of the Beauty Nook came in and saw that the coffin was shut. "My God," she cried, "why can't we *see* her?"

"Calista wanted it that way," Calista told her.

"But her hair is so *perfect*! It's one of the best jobs I've ever done, living or dead, and nobody will ever *see* it."

"Agatha and Frederick saw it. Lillian Kite saw it. I saw it. The Wentworths saw it. She looks lovely."

Next Janet Meers arrived with her son, Stephen, in rubber boots, followed by a number of townspeople. Nora complained to these newcomers about the closed coffin, but found few sympathizers. "What's the big deal?" said Stephen.

"What's the big *deal!*" said Nora, distraught. "Let me assure you, young man, that washing and cutting and setting the hair of the dead is no small job. It's a very, very big deal!"

Samantha the Donut Queen came in and announced that she would serve free coffee when everyone returned from the cemetery. Benji came in from his tavern, looking shaved and shorn and very sad. More Willoughbyites and a few Staggerfordians, crowding into the vestibule, paid their respects to Calista, and when they discovered that the postmistress's body was not to be seen, they went into the church and sat down. Agatha, feeling tired, did the same and overheard a conversation from a nearby pew.

"Dort doesn't look like herself."

"I know. She seems changed."

"Almost like she's shrunk down to Calista's size. Do you suppose grief can do that?"

"Well, obviously it has."

Linda Schwartzman, pushing the coffin slowly up the aisle, was followed by Calista and—substituting for Howie who still hadn't come inside—Congressman Lindquist. Agatha suffered a moment of panic when she realized that the closed coffin hadn't yet brought them quite out of the woods, because there was a good chance that the congressman, being an old family friend, would recognize Calista as Calista.

As Father Healy stepped out into the sanctuary, Howie finally came in and stood beside the front pew until the congressman got up to make room for him beside his sister. Then, after the mass had begun, a latecoming couple slipped into the pew beside Agatha. To her amazement, it was Beverly Bingham. She looked past Beverly to see the man she supposed was her son and was even more surprised to see William Mulholland instead.

Funerals made Agatha angry. In her long life she'd gone through a number of reactions to death—fear, sorrow, indifference, despair—but these days it was making her mad. It was the single major flaw in God's plan, yanking good people away from life, never to be seen again. Good, brainy, bossy, and efficient Dorothy Jean Holister gone from this world forever and ever. It made no sense—unless you equated human beings with ducks and dogs and other animals, one generation dying to make room for the next. No, Agatha never subscribed to that purely scientific way of thinking. She'd always been aware of the great gulf between the highest primates and the wonderful spirit of humankind—men and women capable of invention and reason and laughter and speech. God promised of course that this spirit lived on for eternity in another form, and there have been times when Agatha found comfort in this concept—and she still believed it—but now, drawing closer to death herself, it offered small consolation indeed. Death was simply outrageous.

At Communion time, Agatha remained in her pew, picking this bone with God, which, in her opinion, made her unworthy of the sacrament anyhow, never mind the Big Lie.

Next, when the priest came down to bless the coffin, Agatha was startled to hear him say, "O Lord, may your angels carry our sister Calista into the light of your salvation." And then, in the cemetery at the end of the short Main Street, he inserted Calista's name in his prayers twice as he committed Dort's body to the grave. Agitated, she intercepted him as he was leaving the scene. "Father, you said the wrong name." Her whisper was an urgent hiss. "Three times you said Calista."

"Miss McGee, I wish you'd relax and give God a little credit," he said, laying his long arm across her narrow shoulders. "Surely God knows who died."

This was an unarguable fact, but she felt the need to put in the last word. "Still, I thought you might have left out her name altogether. We shouldn't try to confuse God."

His hearty laugh offended her and she returned to graveside, passing near the congressman and Lolly, who was holding a microphone up to his face. She was buoyed to hear him say, "Oh, yes, Dort will carry on as before; she's already lined up a carrier to take Howie's place on the route, and Howie will help her in the sorting room. She's got it all figured out."

Calista and Lillian were speaking with Beverly. Agatha joined them and said, "How kind of you to come, Beverly. You didn't even know Calista."

"No, but I know her sister," said Beverly, embracing first Calista, then Lillian and Agatha, then Calista again. Janet joined them for another round of hugs. Such was the closeness bred by adversity. "If Sara and Imogene were here, we'd make a complete set," laughed Janet.

Beverly introduced William Mulholland, and although he was

well known to all of them, he gently shook each of the five hands he was offered. After a few moments of small talk, during which Agatha restrained herself from asking about the precise relationship between Beverly and William, the five women moved as one to the hearse and took Linda Schwartzman in their arms as well. The afternoon sun, slanting through a stand of pine trees at the edge of the cemetery, was so remarkably warm that Agatha commented on it, and they all agreed that yes, it felt as if spring was here at last.

THIS YEAR

Calista Holister never wrote letters, so she was surprised to find one in the morning mailbag addressed to her. She also found a windowed envelope addressed to Benji, doubtless another bill from some wholesaler demanding payment. Poor Benji went bankrupt. He'd been gone nearly six months—left his Beer Hall in the middle of the night and was never heard from again. Calista stamped "Return to sender" on his envelope and then opened her own. An invitation from Agatha. She showed it to Frederick, who stood at the sorting table, preparing for his daily delivery. (Her brother Howie had gone down the street for breakfast at Samantha's.) He read it and said, "Yep, she told me about it," and handed it back to her.

"Will you be there?" she asked hopefully. She'd become quite fond of Frederick during the year that she'd been in charge of the mail. Besides, she'd need a ride.

"Nope, not invited."

"But you don't need an invitation to be in your own house."

He looked at it again. "Nope, it's a workday."

"But if you come out and sort, I'll tell Howie to take your route for you."

"No, thanks. I'd just as soon work." He would take the day off if she insisted, but he didn't want to break his record—he hadn't missed a day of work since he became Willoughby's full-time rural mail carrier. Also, he was thinking about Substation Hill, across the line in Gitchee County. At 520 feet above sea level, it was said to be one of the highest points in Minnesota. He loved the view from up there. It was four miles off his mail route, but every day he went out of his way to follow the gravel road up and up, past the sloping fields and woods on the south side of the hill, past the humming wires and towers of the substation that Minnesota Power and Light built there many years ago, and he ate his sack lunch at the very top, looking north across Duck Lake toward Berrington. The city was eighteen miles away, but on clear days, like today, he could see the glint of the chimneys of the packing plant at the near edge of Berrington. On overcast days, he was up among the clouds. Sometimes Samantha used to leave her Donut Shop and join him there—they'd sit in her car and talk, or rather, she'd talk and he'd listen while gazing off into the distance—but since she'd turned her shop into a full-menu cafe, she couldn't get away. Which was okay with him. All she wanted to talk about were kitchen recipes and styles of clothes, and he found all that very tiresome. He'd recommended Substation Hill to Howie, who carried the mail on Saturdays, but Howie wouldn't waste the gasoline it took to get there. Such a difference in people. If Frederick didn't get up the hill five days a week, he felt cheated.

Calista didn't insist. She called Janet Meers and arranged for her to come and pick her up for Agatha's party. While she was on the telephone, Billy Wentworth came in for his mail and called to Frederick through the grill, "Hey, you know what I just heard? There's a new business coming to Willoughby. Some canoe-rental outfit. Going to take over the tavern, they say."

Frederick pondered this news for a few moments, then turned to Billy, who was waiting to tell Calista. "You mean there's money in renting canoes?"

"Guess so. Tourists, they say. For taking rides on the river. That'll bring the number of merchants up to seven. I told Inga pretty soon we'll need a chamber of commerce." Billy laughed. "And guess what Inga says. Inga says pretty soon we're gonna need a city council."

Imogene, home for a late lunch in her sparsely furnished condo, threw the invitation into the wastebasket, telling herself she would ignore it. She dropped a gob of butter into a frying pan and grilled herself a cheese sandwich, all the while calling up in memory the seven women she spent those endless days and nights with during the flood. How could she stand another minute with Agatha's pet, Janet Meers? Janet, after years of driving around in that hideous blue van, had recently got herself a brand new, bright red SUV the size of an army tank, which, according to Imogene's research, sold for just under twenty-four thousand dollars. And not only that, her stupid daughter, Sara, a year ago got her photo in the *Weekly,* having been accepted for admission to some expensive college in the Twin Cities. Well, it was no wonder they were flaunting their wealth; their son, Stephen, home from college, had joined his father's realty firm, and weren't all realtors avaricious cutthroats? Wasn't Beaman Realty charging Imogene eight and a quarter percent interest on this crummy condo in the Marketplace overlooking the garbage cans and dumpsters in the alley behind Main Street?

Then there was Beverly Bingham Mulholland, gone from being the daughter of a murderer and the twice-divorced mother of a schizophrenic son to the high-and-mighty wife of the Staggerford city clerk. Old Mayor Druppers, after a lifetime in office, was retiring this year, and William Mulholland was said to be the leading candidate to succeed him. Of Imogene's thousand and one proofs that life was unfair, nothing could be as conclusive as low-born Beverly Bingham ending up the First Lady of Staggerford.

Unless it was the success of Linda Schwartzman as an undertaker. True, the Case-Schwartzman Funeral and Cremation Service was the only mortuary in town, but that didn't explain why the woman was so popular, why she had that offensive way of strutting when she walked, or why, having been in town scarcely a year, she was recently appointed to the library board and thus became Imogene's overseer.

Then there were the three boring old biddies—Agatha herself, Dort Holister, and Imogene's own benighted mother. *My, my, what a lot of rain we've had in Willoughby this spring. Oh no, it's been awfully dry around Staggerford—it's practically been a drought since the last snow. My stars, I see by the paper that Elizabeth Taylor might get another divorce.* Who'd want to spend a meal in the company of that dismal crew?

Imogene would, as it turned out. Before going back to work she phoned Agatha to accept the invitation. In the first place, it was a free meal, and, second, mixed in among all the banalities spoken at Agatha's table, there were certain to be a few shreds of interesting gossip.

Although there was an invitation on its way to Sara Meers in St. Paul, Janet told her by phone that it was coming. "That's during spring break," said Sara. "So, okay, let's me and you go." She didn't add that her last paper of the year was supposed to be a multiple character sketch. What better place to study multiple characters than in Agatha's house?

"That's what I was hoping you'd say," replied her mother. "Except it's 'you and I.'"

"What is?"

"Let's 'you and I go,' not 'me and you.'"

"How come?"

"Because it's the subject. I, not me. But anyway, how are classes?"

"Mom, it isn't the subject. I said let's. Let's means let us, right?

Me is the object of let. Let us—me and you—go. Let me go, not let I go."

"Okay, Sara, what I want to know is, how's this semester going?"

"English is pretty, like, boring. The prof's a stickler for grammar. That's how I know about subjects and objects and stuff."

"Are you going to pass college algebra this time?"

"No sweat, Mom. I sit next to this, like, really cool guy, his name is Tom? He's been helping me study and stuff. Me and him got Bs on the last test."

Linda Schwartzman was overseeing the remodeling of her house when the invitation arrived in the mail. She found her calendar under the dropcloth on her kitchen counter and happily wrote *AGATHA* on the fourteenth of the month. She was eager to see these women again, particularly the five who hugged her last year in the Willoughby cemetery. She had seldom seen most of them since the Holister funeral, but the memory of that embrace had helped her through some very lonely days.

The invitation, delivered to the Mulhollands' new townhouse near the golf course and country club, provided Beverly with a diversion from her longing. She loved her new husband much more than she had loved the other two, and although they'd been married nearly a year, she still missed him terribly when he was at work. The invitation gave her an idea. Sitting at the patio table, she wrote notes to herself on City of Staggerford stationery—the only paper she could find in the house—concerning her high school classmates. William had kept track of what had become of almost all of them—not that she remembered them all, or cared all that much, but Agatha would be interested.

Nadine Oppegard, to nobody's surprise because she was the class brain, had her doctorate in art history, taught at Dartmouth, and published scholarly articles. Nadine never married, which surprised Beverly because she started going with Peter Gibbon the last few months of school and Beverly had thought they looked ideal as a couple. In choosing a wife, Peter Gibbon, son of Staggerford's football coach, went from the top of the class to near the bottom, marrying the scatterbrained Roxie Booth, whose father, a career army man, had moved her through something like seventeen different schools between kindergarten and her senior year at Staggerford High. Peter was a CPA in Minneapolis. He and Roxie had four kids—two honor students and two uncontrollable delinquents. Sad to say, Roxie was currently undergoing radiation for breast cancer.

But sadder than that was what happened to Jeff Norquist. Talk about an uncontrollable delinquent; Beverly remembered Agatha enumerating the crimes and antics of Jeff Norquist—a stolen car, a drug arrest, etc.—before he left town in the middle of his senior year and became an alcoholic barber in California. On a spring evening three years ago, Jeff came home in a drunken rage and shot his wife and his wife's daughter to death, and then he killed his next-door neighbor who came over to see what all the shooting was about. In return for making a remorseful confession, he was spared from execution and is currently serving three consecutive eighty-five-year sentences in a California prison.

Beverly also noted what became of certain teachers she remembered. Coach Gibbon finished his career in Staggerford and retired to the golf course. Mr. Workman, the principal, succeeded Mr. Stevenson as superintendent, but didn't last long in the job. He went back to being principal at some tiny school in southern Minnesota, and his wife divorced him. Beverly was particularly interested in knowing about Mrs. Workman, the home economics teacher who always went out of her way to try to make Beverly not feel like a misfit in school, but their divorce was the last thing William had heard about them.

At the top of a second page of stationery, she wrote, "What I Wish." Once Beverly started writing, it was hard for her to quit. This had been true since her son had come home from treatment one time years ago with instructions to keep a journal. Because it had been difficult to get him started, Beverly offered to write along with him, and she found herself writing far more than he did. He soon quit altogether, in fact, while Beverly wrote on and on. During the past year Owen had been in and out of two halfway houses in Minneapolis and St. Paul and was currently being treated for alcoholism in a state hospital in Brainerd.

> *I wish time would stop. If things could stay as they are today I'd be the happiest woman in the world. Although he might not have Terry Anderson's sense of humor or B. W. Cooper's affection for my son, William Mulholland is the man for me. People kept telling me not to worry about Owen so much. He's over 21, they said, he's old enough to live his own life, but I couldn't stop worrying. It felt like every time he ran away or went to jail he took my heart with him. But now that William has my heart Owen can't take it away any more.*

Agatha, in her chair by the window, was interrupted in her reading of the *Staggerford Weekly* by a cry of delight from Lillian, who had been going through her mail. "Why, you're throwing a party!" she exclaimed, waving the invitation in the air. "What'll we be serving?"

"I haven't thought about it. Cookies and coffee, I suppose."

"Oh, more than that, Agatha. Let's do it up brown."

"Well, not a dinner, surely."

"Why not? Let's make it a feast. Let's put a ham in the oven."

"But think of the work of it, Lillian." Despite her own improving health—due to cataract surgery and the implanting of a pacemaker below her collarbone—Agatha was continually astounded by Lillian's unflagging energy.

"Ach, hams are easy." Lillian stuffed her mail into her knitting bag and took up her needles. "We'll have ham and sweet potatoes and that broccoli hotdish I got the recipe for off *Lolly Speaking* last week."

Agatha ignored Lillian's recitation of the menu and imagined instead the seven women sitting around her dining room table, and she warmed to the idea, knowing that at least five of them loved her. Janet and Beverly had told her so, and the other three—Lillian, Calista, and Linda Schwartzman—well, she could just tell. She peered over the top of the *Weekly,* watching Lillian knit, and thought how lucky she'd been to have this old friend's steady companionship for eighty years. Of course there were certain complex topics you didn't discuss with Lillian. Religion, for one. Agatha had never mentioned her reason for not receiving Communion each Sunday for a month or more last year. On Ascension Thursday, she finally allowed herself to be talked back to the sacrament by Father Healy, and she'd been receiving ever since—but in her divided heart the matter remained unresolved. If it were true, as her pastor claimed, that her lie was not a mortal sin, then why did she feel guilty every time she joined her fellow parishioners at communion time? On the other hand, if it *were* a mortal sin, then why did Willoughby continue to exist pretty much as it had for the last forty years? She'd been expecting the place to disintegrate as a sign of her guilt. She'd stopped talking about it to Father Healy, ever since he insulted her on the first Sunday of Advent this past winter. After mass she'd gone to him once again with her feelings of shame, and for the first time she told him how she questioned Frederick every time he came home from work, looking for telltale holes in the social and business fabric of Willoughby and what those holes would mean in regard to her Big Lie. Well, so what, if her same old song and dance was becoming tiresome, which it probably was; she could see that—surely that was no excuse for him to tell her, straight out, "Tut, tut, Miss McGee, what an enormous ego one must have to think that one's lie could destroy a whole village." This marked the end of her admiration for Father Healy. Leaving church that morning she thought of the perfect reply—"An enormous ego would not allow one to feel such guilt as I do"—but she didn't want to go back and face him, so she wrote it down and put it in the mail. He never replied.

Perhaps if he'd answered, Agatha might never have consented to cataract surgery or to the emplacement of a pacemaker below her collarbone. To save her sanity, and without Father Healy to spar with, she needed a distraction of some sort to keep her mind off her Big Lie. She settled on reading. Not only the *Staggerford Weekly,* but library books. But of course she needed the eyesight and the energy to read, and thus she went ahead with her medical procedures.

With her eye still on Lillian, who was knitting and knitting, Agatha realized that unresolved, too, in her own mind, was the disagreeable period Lillian went through last year. The woman's spitefulness and impatience went on for six weeks or more, ending shortly after the flood.

"Cranberry sauce is delicious," said Lillian, her eyes on her yarn. "I think we ought to have that, too. Cranberries really dress up a plate."

Lillian's was a grudgelike surliness, and it had Agatha continually going back over her actions, trying to figure out if she was the cause.

"And of course an Easter egg beside each plate, because it will be near Easter. I'll color the eggs."

"Lillian, tell me . . . ," said Agatha tentatively. She'd brought it up two or three times in the past, but to no avail. Lillian always played dumb. She decided to approach it from a new angle. "You've never been sick, have you, Lillian?"

"Sick?"

"Yes, sick. Under the weather."

"Of course I've been sick. We were sick together, remember? We had our tonsils out two days apart."

"We were just girls then. I'm talking about as an adult."

"The year everybody was getting the swine flu, I got that. And I'm pretty stiff in the shoulders. Doc Hammond says it comes from sixty years of bending over my knitting."

"But you've been amazingly healthy overall."

Lillian looked up, as though in amazement. "I have, at that. At least the old ticker keeps on tickin' away."

"And yet at this time last year, around the time of the flood, you weren't acting quite yourself and I'm still wondering why. I mean you seemed—"

"I was mad at Imogene because she wouldn't sell the house like we planned. Just kept living there like a queen till the flood moved her out."

"But why were you taking it out on me?"

"Oh, that was different—that was an addiction problem," was Lillian's flat, clipped answer.

Addiction? But of course, thought Agatha—some pharmaceutical trouble, some sleeping pill or arthritis medicine she got hooked on. Why didn't she think of that? "How did you cure yourself, Lillian? You weren't in treatment."

"No, I wasn't in treatment. The cure was Easter."

"Easter? You mean you prayed?"

"No, I never prayed about it. See, it wasn't your normal type of addiction. I gave up *The National Enquirer* and all papers like that for Lent last year."

"Oh, really?"

"Sure, it was your idea."

"Mine? Not mine surely."

"Yep, you talked me into it in February, and I lasted almost till Easter. I cheated a little at the end because I was suffering withdrawal symptoms." *Click, click* went her needles.

"I'll never give it up again," she added. "Dumbest idea you ever had." *Clickety, clickety-click.*

Compromising, Agatha and Lillian decided to offer a late-morning brunch. Janet phoned the guests, notifying them of the time change. The day dawned foggy and misty, but by midmorning the sun was out. Lillian of course was the first to arrive and immediately started cooking—eggs, sausage, bacon, potatoes, toast—while Agatha made coffee and put the kettle on for tea. Linda Schwartzman and Beverly Mulholland arrived early as well to lend a hand. Beverly drew eight chairs up to the dining room table while Linda set out the plates and silver. Imogene came next, strolling officiously through the house and into the kitchen where she lifted the lids off the pans to inspect the cooking and then retired to the living room couch to await the meal. She was soon joined by Janet and Sara Meers and Calista Holister. Imogene ignored Janet and Calista's attempt to get a conversation started, because she'd decided not to talk either to upstarts or to old people, so they spent an awkward few moments before they were called to the table.

Everyone was impressed, though Imogene and Sara didn't say so, with how well Agatha seemed—her color, her alertness, her strong speech. "Lillian prevailed upon me to see Doctor Hammond for a pacemaker," she explained, taking her place at the head of the table, "and to go to Berrington for cataract surgery. Let us pray." She led them in grace, and then, famished, she dug in.

After the first few bites, there were remarks of satisfaction around the table, and then Beverly said, "I want to get something off my chest before we get carried away." The others were astonished to look up from their plates and see tears in her eyes. "I just want to say how happy I am to be living back in Staggerford, and how good it always makes me feel to be in Agatha's house." She spoke with her eyes on Linda Schawartzman across the table. "Before the flood I hadn't seen Agatha for twenty years and yet I've always thought of her as a second mother. I just want to say thanks."

Calista Holister spoke up then. "Well, she's changed *my* life, let me tell you."

"Here, here, a toast to Agatha," said Linda, and there was a general raising and clinking of coffee mugs and teacups.

"Goodness," said Agatha, "you can't have a proper toast without wine. Janet, would you go into the cellar and bring up a bottle? And the corkscrew from the kitchen."

"Last year's?" asked Janet.

"Yes, I believe that's all there is. Bring up two."

"Oh, she's certainly changed my life," Calista went on. "When I think of how I was before my sister died, why it's kind of a miracle."

Linda snapped her fingers and said, "I've got it. I've been sitting here wondering what's different about you, Ms. Holister, and now I realize what it is. You're not wearing your glasses."

With a sidelong glance at Agatha, Calista said, "That's another way she changed my life. She told me about her eye doctor in Berrington and he brought sight back into my bad eye."

Agatha was no longer surprised so much as she was alarmed by the ease with which Calista could toss off lies like this at the drop of a hat. The woman seemed completely devoid of conscience, and it weighed heavily on Agatha, because she felt responsible. Calista, as Dort, had been so convincing that everyone, including Lillian, believed she was her sister now; and she'd told the story so often about recovering her eyesight that most people—Lillian included—had begun to distrust their memory that Dort had had a glass eye.

"Agatha's been a godsend to me as well," said Linda. "I thought I understood Minnesotans, having grown up in Rookery—how we're all supposed to be so friendly and nice—but Staggerford is a hard town to get acquainted in. If it hadn't been for Agatha I wouldn't have a friend in town."

Janet hurried back to the table with the wine in order to get in her tribute as well. Opening one of the bottles, she reviewed for the others her first experience in this house. "I was pregnant with Stephen, who was about to be born, and there was a blizzard coming, so my dad went to a neighboring farm and called up Agatha— we didn't have a telephone in those days—and he asked if she'd take me in since she lived close to the hospital. I was scared to death of giving birth, and even more frightened of entering the house of the great Agatha McGee."

"Oh, nonsense," said Agatha, pretending to dismiss the idea that she'd ever been the formidable presence she'd worked so hard to maintain.

"No, it's true, Agatha. You'd been my sixth-grade teacher and the only laywoman on St. Isidore's faculty of nuns, so coming into this house was like entering a convent."

To be equated with the Catholic sisterhood, whom she'd never had much respect for, caused Agatha to break out in a hardy laugh. Her mirth was a mystery to the others, but only Sara, storing up details for her term paper, was bold enough to ask, "What are you laughing at?"

"Nuns," said Agatha. "They used to be such odd creatures. Such namby-pambies with one-track minds."

Lillian, to whom Agatha had confided that nuns were a spoiled and overprotected lot, asked, "Aren't they still?"

"Who knows?" Agatha answered. "We haven't seen a nun in Staggerford since Sister Judith Juba left town a dozen years ago. She's taken a job as parish administrator somewhere in the northern reaches of the diocese. I pity the parish."

From the dining room hutch, Janet set out wine glasses, and, pouring a generous amount for each guest, she finished her story. "The blizzard came and went and I still didn't have my baby. I got here on Christmas Eve and Stephen wasn't born until New Year's Day, but I learned more in that week than I ever thought possible. I mean I learned how a house was supposed to be kept. See, I'd grown up with my dad and my sisters in a chaotic household and Agatha's place was so nice and orderly, everything in its place, and I knew that was how I wanted to be."

"But you were naturally orderly, Janet," said Agatha. "You went to work for me at the school and you were efficient from the first day, remember?"

"Sure I remember, but it was during that week in your house that I learned to be efficient. Don't undervalue yourself, Agatha."

Agatha bowed her head humbly, as if waiting for the subject to change. But her humility was false modesty. She knew how powerful her influence had been on Beverly and Calista and Janet. And, for that matter, on scores of her fellow Staggerfordians. She was not one to undervalue herself.

It was Lillian who changed the subject, with this startling question. "Did you know that thirty percent of my housemates are dead?" Pleased to see the surprised look on everyone's face, she went on to explain that last year's evacuation of Sunset Senior had been so traumatic for the residents that 30 percent of them had since died. "Yep, there were seventy-one of 'em hauled off on two buses to Berrington. They slept in a high school gymnasium for four nights. I was there when they were hauled back to Sunset, and you never saw a sorrier looking mess of people getting off a bus in your life. They all looked like they'd been to hell and back, is what they looked like, and before long they started dying off. Addie Simchuck was the first to go—you remember, Agatha, we went to her funeral—and since then there's been fourteen dead and gone. So you see, if Agatha hadn't taken me in I might be pushing up daisies myself."

Agatha, among others, calculated that fifteen dead out of seventy-one residents is closer to 20 percent than 30 percent, but no one corrected Lillian on this. Everyone agreed, however, with Linda Schwartzman's declaration that Lillian was much too vigorous to have died like the others.

"And too bull-headed," said Imogene, smiling bitterly at her bacon and eggs.

There was a pause as the others waited for Lillian to reply to this, but she let it pass in favor of going ahead with her account of death at Sunset. Old Jacob Swenson had died of an infection that started in his ear. Mary Adderly had had "bad dye-beatus." Florence St. Anthony was "full of cancer, just rotten with it—everywhere but her lungs and she used to smoke like a chimney." Nellie Harker "had everything wrong with her—bad heart, dye-beatus, cancer, and foot trouble—it's a wonder she wasn't dead years ago."

"I've never felt stronger myself," said Calista, speaking with her mouth full the way her sister used to. "It isn't only having all of my eyesight back, it's more than that—as Agatha knows." She looked straight at Agatha, as if defying her to reveal their secret.

Lillian continued her recital. "August Hamlin was taken in the night by a huge, huge stroke. Annabelle O'Brien slept away as peaceful as anything."

Calista still held Agatha in her gaze. "Oh yes, Agatha knows all about the change that's come over me."

What sort of monster had she created? Agatha wondered. Calista used to be so meek and mannerly, and now she had taken on the masculine, outspoken ways of her sister. There was aggression in the looks she got from her, as if to say, You're choking on our secret, Agatha McGee, and there's no way you can get rid of it. More than once Agatha had considered coming clean, letting the cat out of the bag, but then she thought of Willoughby and the tenuous existence of the few businesspeople on its short Main Street and she decided once again that the secret was worth keeping for their sake. She'd decided, too, that the less she saw of Calista the better. She regretted the loss of a friend, but understood that it was one of the wages of sin.

Lilllian, as usual, had prepared more than enough food, and the meal ended with everyone sated. Imogene said, "I've got to get back," and hurried off to her afternoon duties at the library, disappointed that there had been so little gossip. Janet's account of her confinement was interesting but it was old news. Walking along in the warm sunshine, Imogene committed to memory the various forms of death that visited Sunset Senior since the flood. Mary Adderly's diabetes. Jacob Swenson's infection. August Hamlin's stroke. These would have to do instead of gossip.

Linda Schwartzman, lingering at the table over Agatha's homemade chokecherry wine, said, "Next month I'll have this group of flood survivors at my house." Janet volunteered for June, and Calista said they'd have to come out to Willoughby in July. Beverly said that she would host them in August. Lillian promised to entertain in the Sunset's dining room for Agatha's birthday in September.

Sara Meers, eager to get home and put her thoughts on paper, urged her mother to leave, and Agatha embraced the two of them as well as Calista at the door. Beverly and Linda stayed to help with the dishes, and when they left Agatha hugged them as well.

"Well, we did all right, if I say it myself," said Lilllian, settling into her customary chair and drawing out her yarn and needles. "Boy, can that Meers girl ever eat. Why, she ate three eggs and at least six strips of bacon."

"Yes," said Agatha absently, standing at the screen door and looking out at her sun-splashed lawn.

"And Dort, do you realize Dort had three helpings of spuds?" Agatha mumbled a response.

"I guess we all ate our share. We used nineteen eggs and two pounds of bacon. You yourself, Agatha, there's nothing wrong with your appetite." Getting no response, Lillian asked, "Are you all right, Agatha?"

She said she was feeling fine. Actually she'd never in her life felt better. She was looking forward to next month and seeing this group of friends again at Linda Schwartzman's house. She was excited to think of gathering at Janet's pretty place on the river and at the several other venues where they would meet between now and fall. Then she would have them here again in October and hoped the cycle kept going. The flood survivors had suffused today's gathering with a warmth such as she hadn't felt since her last pajama party at the age of twelve.